D1516670

# camp ❀ CONFIDENTIAL

Golden Girls

GROSSET & DUNLAP
Published by the Penguin Group
Penguin Group (USA) Inc., 375 Hudson Street,
New York, New York 10014, U.S.A.
Penguin Group (Canada), 90 Eglinton Avenue East, Suite 700,
Toronto, Ontario, Canada M4P 2Y3
(a division of Pearson Penguin Canada Inc.)
Penguin Books Ltd, 80 Strand, London WC2R ORL, England
Penguin Ireland, 25 St Stephen's Green, Dublin 2, Ireland
(a division of Penguin Books Ltd)
Penguin Group (Australia), 250 Camberwell Road, Camberwell,
Victoria 3124, Australia
(a division of Pearson Australia Group Pty Ltd)
Penguin Books India Pvt Ltd, 11 Community Centre,
Panchsheel Park, New Delhi - 110 017, India
Penguin Group (NZ), 67 Apollo Drive, Mairangi Bay,
Auckland 1311, New Zealand
(a division of Pearson New Zealand Ltd)
Penguin Books (South Africa) (Pty) Ltd, 24 Sturdee Avenue,
Rosebank, Johannesburg 2196, South Africa

Penguin Books Ltd, Registered Offices:
80 Strand, London WC2R ORL, England

Cover designed by Ching N. Chan.
Front cover image ©Alloy Photography/Veer Inc.

Library of Congress Control Number: 2006103285

ISBN 978-0-448-44541-0          10 9 8 7 6 5 4 3 2 1

# camp CONFIDENTIAL

## Golden Girls

by Melissa J. Morgan

Grosset & Dunlap

# PROLOGUE

Dear Michael,

   I thought I'd go old-school and write you an actual letter instead of an e-mail this time. Natalie had some of this sweet pink parchment from Kate's Paperie—this cool stationery store in NYC—and I just had to borrow some. I wish I could see the look of surprise on your face when you get a pink letter by snail mail. If any of your friends are around when it arrives, I apologize in advance.

   Camp has been so much better lately. It seems like everyone has just decided to chill after our first couple weeks of, well, total insanity. There haven't been any fights or drama or anything. I know. Sounds impossible, right? But it's true! I'm finally feeling comfortable and having some fun. I never thought I'd say this, but I really feel like I belong here now. Last year I had no idea what I was doing. I may have acted like I was supercool with everything, but really I was like this lost little clueless girl stuck in the middle of the woods. But now, I don't know, I feel like I'm really starting to _get_ camp. The food, the people, the activities. I know who everyone is now, and _where_ everything is. And I love my friends. Camp Lakeview feels sort of like a second home.

Who knows? Maybe I _am_ a camp girl after all! But don't worry, I'll still come back to L.A. at the end of the summer the same girl that left. I haven't lost my mind <u>completely</u>. I could really go for a mango-orange smoothie, a salmon roll, and a deep scalp massage. And a hug from you, of course!

Miss you!
Tori

chapter

ONE

"Yes!"

Tori awoke with a start and tried to pry her eyes open. It couldn't be morning already, could it? Her eyelids were so heavy they felt like rocks, but she managed to blink a few times and look around. A soft, gray light trickled through the cabin windows—definitely not bright enough for morning reveille. But then what had woken her up?

There was a giggle and someone dropped something on the floor across the bunk. Oh, great. Was someone pulling a prank in the middle of the night? Tori *so* didn't want to get involved. Pranks were so childish and pointless. Not to mention potentially damaging to personal property. She rolled over onto her side and lifted her pillow over her head to block out the noise. All she could do was hope it wasn't a silly string or TP attack—something that would get the whole cabin up and screaming. Maybe if she ignored the pranksters, they would just leave her out of it.

"Red team rules!"

Suddenly someone jumped on Tori's bed and flipped her right back onto her back. Tori whipped her pillow away to find Jenna Bloom hovering over her with a wild look in her eyes. Her curly brown hair stuck out in all directions, and she wore a brand-new red T-shirt over her pajama bottoms. Behind her, the rest of the bunk started to rouse and yawn and look around to see what the commotion was. Even though it was pretty dark in the bunk, Tori could see that everyone else was just as confused as she was.

"Are you possessed?" Tori asked.

"Red team is going to kick Blue butt!" Jenna cheered. "And this year I'm not getting injured, so there's gonna be no stopping me! Woo-hoo!"

*Oh, God. Color War!* Tori thought, her brain finally waking up enough to figure out what was going on. Jenna shook Tori a few times, chanting, "Red! Red! Red!" Then she climbed the bunk ladder to taunt Alex Kim.

"How do you know you're on Red?" Alex asked, fully alert as she climbed out of bed.

"T-shirts in our cubbyholes, baby! Color War's early this year! Red all the way! Woo-hoo!"

Jenna was now in the center of the cabin doing a sort of jerky, bizarro dance, like she was trying to bring on the rain or something. Tori rolled her eyes at Natalie Goode, who was just stretching her arms over her head in her own bed. Natalie shook her head in reply, clearly amused. Everyone knew Jenna lived for Color War. The previous summer she had been all but shut out of participating because she had hurt her ankle

9

right before the yearly ritual began. Tori remembered feeling badly for Jenna, but also a little bit jealous of her. Tori would love to be excused from Color War. The competition wasn't exactly Tori's cup of decaf chai tea. She had never been much of an athlete. Not like some of the other girls in her bunk. Tori was more into fashion and makeup and celebrity gossip than sports.

"I'm on Blue!" Alex announced, finding a new T-shirt in her cubby and yanking it on. Her dark hair staticked out and she smoothed it with one hand.

"I'm on Red!" Valerie exclaimed, high-fiving with Jenna. The beads at the ends of her multiple braids clicked as she lifted her hair out from the neck of her tee.

As the rest of the girls yanked out their T-shirts, Tori reluctantly crawled out of bed. She was aching to go back to sleep, but she didn't want to be labeled as a party pooper. Halfway across the room, Natalie tossed Tori a blue T-shirt. It had that crisp, brand-new cotton smell. It said CAMP LAKEVIEW in small letters above the pocket, and COLOR WAR in huge letters on the back.

"We're both on Blue!" Natalie announced, pulling her own shirt on over her head.

"Sweet," Tori replied. At least with Nat on her team she'd have someone like herself to bond with. And maybe laugh with over the silliness of the whole thing.

"Yeah, Blue team!" Grace called out, her red hair tucked into the collar of her new shirt. She slapped Tori's hand so hard it stung. "Blue team rules! Blue team rules! Blue team rules!"

Gaby, who was also wearing blue, joined Grace's chant. Candace stuck her arms through the holes of her own blue T-shirt and came over to stand quietly near Natalie and Tori. Candace was normally shy and usually either stayed quiet or repeated everything the other girls said. She had never been the chanting type.

"*Red* team rules! *Red* team rules! *Red* team rules!" Jenna shouted over Grace and Gaby. Priya, Valerie, Brynn, and Chelsea all joined in with her. Soon Alex came in on the Blue side, and finally Natalie joined in as well, clearly not wanting to be outshined by Red. Tori simply smiled and leaned back against Grace's bunk bed behind her. She just did not have that competitive streak. Apparently Alyssa, who was on the Red team, didn't have one, either. She had put on her red shirt and crawled right back into bed.

"Red team rules!"

"*Blue* team rules!"

"Red team!"

"Blue team!"

"Red!"

"Blue!"

"Girls!"

All the lights in the cabin flicked on and everyone instantly fell silent. Tori turned around to find Belle, the counselor for bunk 5A, standing in the doorway between her room and the main room, her short dark hair sticking straight up in the back. She wore her usual black tank top and gray boxer shorts, and had a bit of black mascara smudged under her eyes. Not a good look for her.

"Okay, it is *way* too early for this. Would you kindly quiet down and go back to bed?" Belle said through her teeth. "I stayed up late waiting for you all to fall asleep so I could put your T-shirts in your cubbies, and I'm tired. And tiredness makes me *really* grumpy!"

"We noticed," Chelsea said under her breath, earning a round of laughter from the other girls.

"Now I want perfect silence until reveille, which isn't for another . . . hour and a half," Belle said, checking her digital watch. "Is that understood?"

Belle was definitely a no-nonsense type of counselor.

"Yes," everyone grumbled.

"Good."

Belle turned around and seconds later her cot squeaked under her weight. Everyone, including Tori, giggled through the tension as they returned to their beds. Tori climbed under the covers, but after a few minutes, whoops and hollers could be heard from other bunks all over the camp. Everyone was waking up early and finding their T-shirts. Even in her anti-Color-War state of mind, a shiver of anticipation shot through Tori.

"I love Color War so much," Jenna said dreamily.

Everyone laughed. So much for perfect silence.

△ ▽ △

The sun was up and shining, and all of bunk 5A was already gathered in a circle in the center of the cabin later that same morning—red shirts on one side, blue on the other—when Natalie finally found the bottle of nail polish she was looking for and joined them. She plopped down between Grace and Alex, and placed her foam toe separators on each foot.

"What're you doing?" Gaby asked her. "Are you ever *not* primping?"

"It's for team spirit!" Natalie replied.

She produced the bottle of blue glitter polish from behind her back and quickly went to work on her toes.

"Wow! Nice touch!" Grace said. "But how'd you know you'd be on Blue?"

"I didn't. I have red, too," Natalie said. "But personally, I like blue *so* much better," she said pointedly, grinning at the Red side of the circle. "It's so much more original."

"Ugh! Natalie, could you get rid of that stuff? It's stinking up the place!" Jenna said, waving a hand in front of her face.

"It never bothered you before," Natalie said.

"It's not the nail polish. It's the *color* that stinks!" Jenna replied.

The whole Red team cracked up and Natalie went back to her pedicure. "Ha ha. Hope for your sake they don't have a stand-up competition this year."

"Ooooh!" the Blue team chorused. Grace and Alex high-fived over Natalie's head. Natalie smirked. After three summers here, she was starting to get good at this trash-talking thing.

"Okay, ladies, let's call this little meeting to order!" Belle announced, stepping out of her room with her clipboard. She was wearing a red T-shirt. The bunk's CIT, Clarissa, wore a blue shirt and stood next to Belle with two cloth bags in her hands—one red and the other blue. This was new. Natalie was officially curious, and she could tell by the looks on her friends' faces that they were as well.

"First, thank you for going back to sleep earlier this morning . . . even if it did take you another half hour to quiet down," Belle said, earning a few giggles from the bunk. "Now that you all know which teams you're on, I have some Color War–related announcements."

"Color War! Yeah!" Jenna cheered.

"I appreciate the enthusiasm, Jenna, but if you keep doing that I might never get through this," Belle said with a laugh.

"Sorry," Jenna said, pressing her lips together.

"Okay, since there are so few fifth-division campers this year, you guys will be combining with the sixth-division girls for some of the events," Belle said. "Only those which require large teams like soccer and capture the flag. For the rest of the events, you'll be strictly fifth division."

A murmur of interest ran through the circle. The sixth-division girls? They were so cool. And so . . . intimidating.

"Dr. Steve has also decided that this year, each team in each division will have a captain."

"Cool! I'm in!" Jenna announced, raising her hand.

"I'll do it!" Alex chimed in as well.

"Wait a second. What if I want to do it?" Gaby said.

Belle held up her hand. "In order to avoid

having this turn into a popularity contest, I've decided to choose captains based on chance. The last thing this bunk needs is more rivalry."

Natalie nodded her head in agreement as she moved to her pinky toe. Since the very first day of camp this year, she and her bunkmates had been feuding about one thing or another, and only recently had everyone sort of calmed down and started to get along. If they voted for captains now, everyone would get upset all over again.

"So, in each of these bags there are six paper circles, five black and one gold," Belle said. Clarissa stepped forward and placed the red bag in front of Jenna and the blue bag in front of Candace. "Whoever picks the gold circle from each bag will be your captain."

"Go ahead! Pick!" Clarissa instructed.

Candace took a deep breath and reached into the blue bag. She came out with a black circle and sighed, clearly relieved. She handed the blue bag to Alex. Alex closed her eyes and yanked out . . . a black circle as well. She shrugged and gave the bag to Natalie. Nat quickly capped her nail polish, reached into the bag, and mixed up the circles inside. Then she grabbed one and pulled it out. Another black circle. She handed the bag to Grace.

"Come on, gold! Come on, gold!" Grace said. She reached in and yanked out . . . a black circle.

"Well, it's one of you two," Natalie said to Gaby and Tori. Secretly she was hoping Tori would get the gold. Gaby was bossy enough as it was. If she got to be captain, her head might swell to the point of explosion.

Tori reached into the bag and pulled out . . . the gold circle!

"Nice!" Natalie cheered.

"Captain Tori!" Grace cried out.

"Uh . . . great," Tori said, forcing a smile.

Gaby huffed and dropped back onto her elbows.

"Yeah, Priya!" Brynn cheered on the other side of the circle. Natalie glanced over at the Red side and saw Priya clutching the gold circle. She was grinning from ear to ear.

"Good. Our captains will be Tori for Blue and Priya for Red," Belle said, making a note on her clipboard. "Congratulations, ladies. Now let's do our electives, everyone. I'll be in my room. Alyssa? You're first."

As Alyssa got up to find out what her new elective activities would be, the Blue team gathered around Tori to congratulate her. Tori smiled and thanked them all, but Natalie could tell she wasn't all that psyched.

"Hey, Nat! Can I get some of that nail polish?" Tori asked suddenly, grabbing Natalie's arm. She practically yanked Nat outside onto the front porch, Natalie hobbling awkwardly in her toe separators. A bunch of third-division girls walked by with their counselor on their way to the flagpole. Soon more campers joined them. It was still a bit early, but apparently everyone was psyched to get to the Color War opening ceremony.

"What's the matter?" Natalie whispered the second the screen door slammed behind them.

"I can't be captain!" Tori replied. "I don't even

like Color War, and I stink at sports."

"Better not let Jenna hear you dissing Color War. She'll disown you for good," Natalie said. She sat down on the front steps to finish her toenails as more campers trailed by, some already chanting for their teams.

"I'm serious, Natalie. I have nothing to bring to the team. I'm sure someone else would be better," Tori said, leaning back on the wooden railing that surrounded the porch. "Like Alex. She's done, like, a million of these things. Or Gaby. She *loves* to tell people what to do. And they both wanted it. Do you think Belle would let me give it to someone else?" she asked, looking down at her crumpled gold circle.

"I don't know. She seemed pretty serious about doing it by chance," Natalie said. "If you switch, then the Red team might want to switch. It'll be a whole big mess."

Tori groaned and pulled her long blond hair forward over her shoulder. She lifted a big chunk and started to chew on it—something Natalie knew she only did when she was really upset, and *never* in public.

"Tori, don't worry about it. You're going to make a great captain. You just have to get in the spirit of things," Natalie said, getting up and putting her arm around her friend. Instantly, Tori dropped the hair. "Believe me, I did *not* get Color War my first year here, either, but now I kind of like it. Maybe you can, too, if you try. And if you need any help, I'm there. We'll do it together."

"Yeah?" Tori asked, brightening slightly.

Natalie felt that warm and fuzzy feeling she

always got in her chest when she helped someone out. "Definitely. What're best friends for?"

"Hey! 5A! Nice toenails."

Lainie Wilcox, the single coolest girl in the sixth division, paused at the foot of the steps with two of her friends behind her, all of them wearing blue T-shirts. For a long moment, Natalie was completely speechless. She had known who Lainie was since her first summer here. *Everyone* knew who Lainie was. With her light brown hair, perpetual healthy tan, double-pierced ears, and serious athletic ability, Lainie *was* Camp Lakeview. She was a star. And now that she was in sixth division, she practically ran the place. But she never lowered herself to talk to anyone younger than her, which was why Natalie was so stunned.

"You . . . you like them?" she asked.

"Totally. When I walked out of our bunk, I saw you over here and I *thought* you were giving yourself a pedicure, but I had to come over and see for sure. I'm glad you're on team Blue, Goode," Lainie said. "We could use a little originality on our side."

Natalie and Tori exchanged a look. Not only was Lainie talking to Natalie, but she knew her name. *And* she was complimenting her. It was as if the entire Camp Lakeview universe had just been turned on its head.

"So . . . you coming to opening ceremonies or are you just gonna stand there all day?" Lainie asked, earning a small laugh from her friends.

"We have to wait for the rest of the cabin," Tori said.

Lainie smirked, as if what Tori had said was

childish, but she nodded. "Okay. Come find us when you get down there, Goode," she said, looking right at Natalie as if Tori wasn't there. Then she and her friends turned around and sauntered off. Natalie could barely breathe.

"Okay. What just happened here?" she asked.

"I think Lainie Wilcox just invited you to hang out with her," Tori replied, just as shocked.

"Nah. Not possible," Natalie said, blushing with pleasure nonetheless. "Come on. Let's go tell Belle everyone's already on their way."

Suddenly Natalie couldn't wait to get down to the flagpole. Because even though part of her thought there was no way Tori was right, she had to find out for sure. If the coolest girl in camp wanted to be her friend, she was not going to let that opportunity pass her by.

chapter

# TWO

"I actually kind of like Color War," Natalie said as she and the rest of her team made their way to the flagpole. She scanned the crowd for signs of Lainie and her friends, but didn't see them. All around her, kids in red and blue chanted and sang, trying to out-cheer one another. A bunch of first-division Blue team girls had made themselves into a chain, holding hands, and were weaving in and out of the crowd. Laughter and shouting filled the air. "It's like the whole camp is jacked up on Red Bull or something."

"I know! That's exactly what it's like. Like the whole camp is on Red Bull," Candace said, her eyes shining.

"That's one way of putting it," Tori said. A couple of fourth-division boys narrowly missed crushing her foot as they ran past, and she paused for a moment to catch her breath.

"Have you seen any of the fifth-division guys?" Alex asked, wrapping her sleek hair back in a short ponytail as they walked.

"Why? Wondering what team Adam is

on?" Grace teased, elbowing Alex in the side.

"Maybe," Alex said, blushing. She and Adam, Jenna's twin brother, had been doing the boyfriend/girlfriend thing since last summer.

"You do know that if he's on Red, he's officially the enemy," Gaby put in. "And there's no talking to the enemy."

"Like we're not going to talk to the other girls in our bunk for the whole week," Grace said, rolling her eyes.

"Yeah. We have to talk to the other girls in our bunk," Candace said.

"Not any more than absolutely necessary," Gaby said. "Come on, you guys! This is war. Get in the spirit!"

Natalie laughed. "Maybe Gaby's right. But instead of, you know, freezing out our friends, maybe we should take this opportunity to get to know some of the Blue teamers in the other divisions."

"Like Lainie Wilcox?" Tori asked, raising an eyebrow.

"Not *just* her," Natalie said.

Just then, the girls came upon the back end of the crowd gathered around the flagpole, and Natalie couldn't help but grin. The whole dirt field was awash with color, Blues on the right, Reds on the left. Dr. Steve stood in the center, right in front of the flagpole, wearing a T-shirt that was red on the left, blue on the right—two T-shirts sewn together, actually. He'd done the same with his shorts, his hat, *and* his shoes—one red, one blue. He looked ridiculous, but that was kind of the point.

"Welcome, Lakeview campers, to Color War!" he shouted into his megaphone.

The whole place erupted in cheers.

"One! Two! Three! Four! We want Color War! Five! Six! Seven! Eight! We don't want to wait!" the counselors began to chant. "One! Two! Three! Four! We want Color War! Five! Six! Seven! Eight! We don't want to wait!"

Gradually all the campers started to chant with them, their voices filling the clear air. Natalie threw her head back and joined in until the whole camp had gone through the chant three times. Grace and Alex even do-si-doed to the beat while they chanted. Then everyone hooted and hollered until Dr. Steve got the whole place under control again. He started going on about the rules and Natalie tuned him out. She'd heard this speech before. Instead, she decided to use this time to look around for Lainie and her friends. She stood on her toes and craned her neck, checking out the Blue side of the flagpole. Finally, she found them, standing under the shade of some trees at the edge of the clearing, looking at a magazine. There were five girls total in blue, including Lainie, and none of them were paying any attention to Dr. Steve, either.

"I'll be right back," Natalie whispered to Tori.

Tori looked past Nat and saw Lainie and the others. "You're going over there?"

"Yeah. I think so. Wanna come?" Natalie asked, thinking a little moral support might help.

"They didn't ask me. They just asked you,"

Tori stated.

"I'm sure they won't care," Natalie replied.

"Lainie Wilcox won't care. Yeah, right," Tori said with a laugh. "I've only been here two years and even I know she wants things the way she wants them. Don't worry. I'll still be here when you get back." She patted Natalie on the back with a smile and Natalie grinned in return.

"Okay. Wish me luck," Natalie said.

"Good luck!" Tori replied.

Natalie took a deep breath and wove through the crowd toward Lainie and her friends. Her heart pounded with nervousness as she approached. What if she'd gotten the message wrong? What if Lainie didn't actually want to hang out with her? This could be social suicide.

*They're just girls,* she reminded herself as she reached the edge of the crowd. *Next year you'll be them. Basically.*

The moment she was in the clear, two of the girls looked up—two that hadn't been with Lainie earlier outside bunk 5A. One had long jet black hair in braids. The other had a short blond 'do. Both greeted Natalie with seriously obnoxious expressions.

"What do *you* want?" the blond girl asked.

"Omigod, are you wearing white Juicy shorts?" the other said. "Those'll get ruined in about five seconds."

"Yeah. This is Lakeview. Not Park Avenue."

Natalie felt as if she'd just been slapped. Her cheeks burned like mad. Okay, so maybe this had been a huge mistake.

"Hey. Back off, girls," Lainie said, stepping forward. "I invited her over here."

"You did?" one of the girls asked automatically. The other girl smacked her arm as if she couldn't believe the girl had talked back to Lainie.

"Yes, I did," Lainie snapped. "I think it's cool she has her own style."

Suddenly the two mean girls looked sorry they had ever opened their mouths. Natalie tried not to smile too widely. Now *that* was power.

"So, your first name's Natalie, right?" Lainie asked. "Natalie Goode? You're Tad Maxwell's daughter."

Natalie's heart dropped. Of course. Lainie only knew her because her dad was a famous actor. Why hadn't she thought of that before?

"That's *you?*" the blond girl said, her mouth dropping open.

"Very cool," the other girl said.

*Wow. Dramatic turnaround,* Natalie thought. She looked at Lainie, who seemed to be assessing her. Was she going to ask Nat to get her father's autograph for her now? Oh, how Natalie hated this part.

"That must be really hard, having someone famous in your family," Lainie said finally.

"Hard? *Please!* She can have anything she wants!" the dark-haired girl said.

"Who cares, Daniella? That's just stuff," Lainie said. She glanced at Natalie. "I bet people are always trying to get you to do things for them. I bet you never know who your real friends are."

Slowly, Natalie smiled. In her entire life, no one had ever figured that out so quickly. Even Nat's friends in her bunk had been totally starstruck back when they'd first found out that Natalie was the daughter of the biggest action movie star in the universe. It had taken them forever to understand that there were drawbacks to all that attention.

"These two rudes are Patty and Daniella," Lainie said, pointing her thumb at the two tormentors. "And this is Liliko and Trish." She gestured to a tall Asian girl with purple streaks in her hair, and a sort of chubby girl with freckles and long red hair down her back—the two girls who had been with her earlier.

"Hey," they both said, offering up smiles.

"Hi," Natalie responded.

"So, Nat, Liliko just got the back-to-school *Teen Vogue*, and we're picking out first day of school outfits," Lainie said, hooking her arm around Natalie's shoulders. "I bet you know all about fashion, so what do you think? Is orange really the new black?"

Natalie laughed as Liliko opened the magazine to a fashion spread. She could hardly believe her luck. This morning she had woken up just a regular fifth-division girl, and now, suddenly, she had an in with the sixth-division girls. With Lainie Wilcox. All because of a little blue glitter nail polish. Color War was even cooler than she thought.

▲ ▲ ▲

There was way too much noise. Too much cheering, too much splashing, too many voices shouting. Tori squeezed the pen and paper she had in her hands. She closed her eyes and tried to block it all out, but it was no use. Gaby, after all, was yelling directly in her ear.

"I totally think I should be in the tube," Gaby said. "It's the most important part of the race."

"Uh, no. It's not," Alex countered, hands on hips. "And even if it *was*, why does that mean *you* should do it?"

"Yeah! Why does that mean you should do it?" Candace echoed.

"I'll do whatever, Tori! I'll get wet! Or not! I don't care!" Grace offered enthusiastically.

Tori took a deep breath and stared at the water. It was the first event of Color War and already she was at a loss. Everyone else on the docks was cheering their heads off for the fourth-division boys, who were in the middle of their relay race. She watched as a spiky-haired boy jumped in his kayak and started speeding across the lake. There were four vessels in all. An inner tube, a canoe, a paddleboat, and a kayak. Tori had to figure out which of her teammates would man each boat. The tube would go first, making one cross of the lake. The moment it touched the opposite dock, the canoe would take off. Then the paddleboat, followed by the kayak. Unfortunately, everyone had an opinion on who should do what.

"I'll do the inner tube," Alex said. "I'm a strong swimmer."

"Stronger than *me*?" Gaby huffed.

Behind her, on the next dock, a loud whistle split

the air. Tori turned to see that Priya had just shut her own team up with that one sharp noise.

"Okay, Brynn and Jenna in the paddleboat. Alyssa and Val in the canoe. I'll take the kayak, and Chelsea, you're in the tube. Got it?" Priya said.

"Got it," the red team chorused.

"Hands in!" Priya shouted.

And the entire Red team gathered in a circle to put their hands in the center. Meanwhile, team Blue was slowly melting down.

"Just make a decision, Tori. It's up to you," Alex said.

"I don't see why it has to be up to her—"

Tori looked around for Natalie. After all, Nat had said she would help her out with anything—that they'd do this captain thing together. And she needed her help right now—big-time. But when she finally found her friend in the crowd, she was at least a hundred yards and a hundred *people* away, chatting with Lainie Wilcox and a bunch of other sixth-division girls.

*Come on, Natalie. Remember your promise,* Tori urged silently. But Natalie just kept gabbing away. Apparently she was not receiving Tori's telepathic message. She was on her own here.

"Tori—"

"You have to—"

"It's gonna start—"

"Okay! Fine!" Tori shouted. She used Alex's back for a table and scribbled out her team on the paper she'd been given. "Grace is in the tube, Nat is in the kayak, Candace and Alex in the paddleboat, and Gaby and me in the canoe. Okay?"

They all fell silent, and Tori felt proud of herself. She'd done it. She'd taken control! So why didn't anyone else look all that pleased?

Corey, one of the boys' counselors, darted over. He'd used white tape to spell out the words "Blue Rulez!" on the front of his blue shirt. "Hey! I need your final list."

Tori handed it over and Corey ran off with it to Dr. Steve. Just then, the fourth-division boys finished and everyone cheered for the Red team, who had won by inches. Natalie came bounding up and jumped into the circle, all smiles.

"So! What's the deal?" she asked.

Tori was relieved to see her. At least she knew *Natalie* would support her.

"You're on the last leg. In the kayak," Tori told her.

Natalie's face completely fell. "The kayak? I've never even been *in* a kayak before!"

"What? How could you be at camp for three years and never be in a kayak?" Tori asked, her heart clenching.

"I've never had water sports as an elective!" Nat cried.

"Oh, God! Maybe I can still change—"

At the top of the docks, Dr. Steve lifted his microphone. "Fifth-division girls! In your boats!"

"Come on, Brynn! Paddle, Jenna!" Priya shouted from the dock as her friends sped toward the far side of the lake in their paddleboat. The rest of her team, Chelsea, Valerie and Alyssa, were all on the far shore, having finished their legs of the race, and they were cheering as well. Priya saw Brynn glance over her shoulder at the Blue team and laugh, which made Priya stifle a grin. Team Blue was *miles* behind. There was no way Red could lose at this point, but Priya kept shouting, anyway.

"Go! Go! Go!"

Finally the paddleboat reached the dock on the far side of the lake. Jenna stood halfway up and strained to grab the red flag that dangled from the ladder on their side of the dock. Jenna thrust the flag into the air, which was Priya's cue to go. Heart pounding, Priya jumped into the kayak, grabbed the oar, and took off.

"Go, Priya! Yeah!" Valerie and the other members of the Red team cried. The race was almost over. It was up to Priya to finish off the

Blue team.

Paddling hard, Priya concentrated on her rhythm. Right, left, right, left. She was halfway across the lake when she saw Alex lift the blue flag in the air and the Blue team let out a cheer. Apparently, Natalie had started off in her kayak.

Just for good measure, Priya glanced over her shoulder to see how far behind Natalie was. Her jaw dropped. Natalie was struggling with her oar, turning the kayak around in a wide, awkward circle.

"Straighten out! Straighten out!" Gaby shouted from the shore, as a bunch of kids along the shoreline started to laugh.

Priya was no longer paddling, but drifting forward when Natalie finally seemed to get control of herself. Unfortunately, as soon as she started paddling, she took off in the wrong direction.

"Ack! How do you control this thing!?" Natalie shouted, her voice carrying over the water.

More kids joined the crowd at the edge of the water and the laughter grew. Natalie was heading toward the east side of the lake and the swimming area. She couldn't be on a more ridiculous course.

*I should go help her*, Priya thought, her heart going out to her friend. She knew that *she* would never be able to handle the entire camp pointing and laughing at her.

"Priya! Come on! What're you doing?" Chelsea shouted from the shore. "GO!"

"Row! Row! Red!" a bunch of Red team members started chanting. "Row! Row! Red!"

The chant got under Priya's skin and energized her. This *was* war, after all. She stuck her paddle in the water and pushed, quickly regaining her rhythm. Within two minutes she had reached the other side of the lake, and the entire Red team erupted in crazy-loud cheers and applause. Chelsea even hugged Priya when she got out of her kayak.

"Nice work, Captain," Belle said, coming over to pat Priya on the back.

"Thanks," Priya said.

That's when she saw Tori standing a few feet away, hanging her head, with her hands over her eyes. Natalie was drifting toward shore now, clear on the other side of the lake. The Blue team wasn't even going to finish.

"I don't know why Tori split up her team that way," Chelsea said rather loudly. "Everyone knows Alex is the strongest swimmer in the fifth division. I would have put her in the tube and Candace in the kayak. I mean, it's not rocket science."

"Chelsea," Priya scolded, hoping Tori wouldn't hear.

Chelsea gulped and looked at the team guiltily. "Sorry. Forgot to do the whole 'think before I speak' thing there."

Priya took a deep breath and walked over to Tori. "It's just the first event," she said, placing her hand on Tori's back. "You have tons of time to catch up."

"Thanks," Tori said weakly.

"Good sportsmanship, girls," Belle told them, smiling proudly. "Nice job."

Priya smiled. Dr. Steve blew the whistle, signaling the end of the race. "Fifth-division girls, Blue, I'm afraid you're disqualified," he said into his megaphone. The entire Red team cheered. "Will someone go help Natalie Goode out of her kayak?" Dr. Steve requested.

Tori's shoulders slumped and she turned around, disappearing into the crowd.

"Should I go talk to her?" Priya asked Belle.

"No. Give her some time to shake it off. She'll be all right," Belle replied.

But the rest of the Blue team were grumbling amongst themselves, while Natalie struggled to beach her kayak on the other side of the lake. Tori's captainship was not off to the best start.

▲ ▲ ▲

*Oh, why can't a huge whirlpool open up in the middle of the lake and just suck me in now?* Natalie thought as she drifted toward the rocky shore next to the diving boards. All along the beach, other campers from the Red team—mostly guys—were waiting for her and cheering her arrival. And why not? Her lack of kayaking ability had just won them the event. They had all left the docks just to welcome her to the entirely wrong part of the lake. Boys were so evil.

Finally, the bottom of the kayak scratched along the bottom of the lake and stopped. Natalie looked around. How was she supposed to get out of this thing without getting soaked? Answer, no-how. This was going to be interesting.

"Hey! Team Blue! You're about a zillion miles off

course!" some kid shouted.

"Need a compass?" another joked. "I mean, the lake isn't that wide, but if you need one . . ."

"Ha ha," Nat said under her breath. She tossed her oar into the water, braced her hands on either side of the hole she was sitting in, and hoisted herself up. The second she did, she felt her balance shift and her heart swooped. Suddenly the trees on the shore tilted and Natalie held her breath. She was going over.

The water was cold and it instantly soaked her shorts and shirt. She was upside down under the water and it was so shallow that her head hit the floor of the lake. Nat tried to push herself away from the kayak, but her foot was stuck.

That was when panic set in. She flailed her arms and tried to sit up, but she couldn't get into a position to reach the surface.

*Omigod! I'm drowning! I'm drowning!* Natalie thought wildly.

Then a strong hand closed around her upper arm and pulled her up. Natalie gasped for air and coughed.

"Are you okay?"

Natalie shoved her matted hair out her eyes and blinked them open. Standing before her with his hand still on her arm was the most beautiful sixth-division boy in all of Camp Lakeview. Natalie had seen him at mealtime and had always thought he was cute, but never remotely imagined she would ever talk to him. He had shaggy blond hair, blue eyes, a deep tan, and wore a silver medallion around his neck on a leather cord. As an added bonus, he was sporting a Blue team

T-shirt as well.

And now here he was saving her from a ridiculous near-drowning in two feet of water while she stood in front of him looking like a wet dog. Fabulous. At least she'd worn waterproof mascara.

"I'm fine, thanks," she said, trying to tuck her sandy, knotted hair behind her ears. She grabbed the hem of her T-shirt and wrung it out. That was when she noticed that he was standing with his sneakers immersed in the water.

"Oh, God. You ruined your treads for me!" Nat exclaimed.

"Small price," he said with a grin. "Come on."

He took her hand and helped her up the shore to where the other guys were standing, still laughing.

"Nice navigating, Blue," one of the guys in red said. "You couldn't find due north on a compass."

"Kind of like you haven't found a comb or a mirror since you've been here?" Natalie shot back.

"Oh! Nice one!" Nat's lifesaver cheered, holding out his hand to be slapped.

Natalie happily obliged. "Thanks."

"A girl who's mastered the perfect comeback. I like it," he said, eyeing her with appreciation.

Natalie grinned as the tormentor touched his knotted hair. She wasn't usually big on insulting people, but he'd started it, and apparently the beautiful boy liked her attitude.

"Sheesh, Logan. You don't have to take her side," one of the guys complained. "We're just having a little fun."

*Logan. What a cool name,* Natalie thought, the butterflies in her stomach whirling and twirling.

"And she had fun right back. No harm, no foul. Come on. Let's go find you a towel," Logan said to Natalie.

"That sounds perfect." Natalie was full-on blushing as she fell into step with Logan and headed back toward the rest of the camp. Maybe this chance meeting could be the start of something amazing—something that would take the sting out of embarrassing herself in front of everyone. A girl could dream.

△ △ △

Tori leaned back against a wide tree trunk near the back of the crowd at the docks, wishing she could disappear. She had made basically the worst decisions ever when it came to her relay team. Her friends were right. Candace would have been better in the canoe or the kayak, and Grace had been really slow in the tube. And not only had her team lost, but Natalie had been totally humiliated.

She wondered where Nat was now. Tori had a feeling she owed her friend a big apology. Of course, if Natalie had been there to help like she'd promised, the girl never would have ended up in the kayak in the first place.

*I thought we were going to do this together,* Tori thought, her heart heavy. *Then Lainie swoops in and says "hi," and suddenly Natalie is nowhere to be found.*

Soon Alex, Grace, Gaby, and Candace appeared, weaving their way out of the crowd. The first thing

Tori noticed was that Natalie wasn't with them. The second was that they all looked very serious. Tori's heart skipped a beat. What were they going to do, overthrow her already? Actually, maybe that wouldn't be the worst idea.

"Hey," Alex said tentatively.

"Hi," Tori said.

"We just wanted to tell you not to be upset," Grace said, slinging her arm over Tori's shoulder. "It was just one event. We'll do better on the next one."

"Yeah. We'll do better on the next one," Candace added.

"It was a lame way to start off Color War, anyway," Gaby said. She yanked a leaf off a nearby tree and shredded it into tiny bits. "They should've done something easier."

"Totally," Alex agreed.

Tori felt the weight around her heart lighten a bit. At least her friends were trying to make her feel better, even if they did still seem disappointed. "Thanks, you guys."

"Sixth-division girls! In your boats!" Dr. Steve announced on his microphone.

Just then, Lainie, who was the captain of sixth-division Blue, shoved her way through the crowd with the rest of her team in tow. She looked Tori up and down like Tori was a wad of lake scum.

"Nice way to crash and burn, fifth," Lainie said snottily. "Now you get to watch how it *should* be done."

Tori felt like someone had just punched her in

her already weak stomach. Her mouth dropped open and a small, squeaking noise came out. Who the heck did this girl think she was? Tori knew that Lainie had a reputation for thinking she was oh-so-great, but she was also supposed to be Miss Camp Spirit. She shouldn't be putting other people down.

"We're on the same team, you know!" Alex shouted after Lainie. But it was too late. Lainie had already moved on and had disappeared into the crowd at the docks.

"That girl is *so* overrated," Gaby grumbled, kicking at a stone on the ground in front of her.

"Why would she say that? I thought this whole Color War thing was supposed to be about teamwork," Tori said.

"As if," Grace said. "If there's one thing everyone at Lakeview has known about Lainie Wilcox since the beginning of time, it's that she's only on one person's team."

"Her own," Alex and Grace finished together.

chapter

# FOUR

Before lunch, Belle allowed Natalie to take a little extra time in the bathroom to recover from her unexpected dunk in the lake. Nat dried her hair with her hair dryer and put on a touch of eyeliner and lip gloss, just in case she saw Logan at the mess hall. She didn't want him thinking she always looked like a lake monster. With any luck, his second impression of her would be better than his first. Although he did seem to like her, even with the dripping clothes and knotted hair. On their way to find her a towel, he had laughed at all her jokes and had touched her back twice. That had to mean something.

Natalie grabbed her sweatshirt and jogged out of the cabin. There were still some straggling groups making their way toward the mess hall. Up ahead, a group of first-division girls played patty-cake games while they walked. Natalie smiled, remembering when she was obsessed with those games. Then, just as she was about to pass the girls by, one of them stepped sideways on a rock and hit the ground hard.

"Ow! Owwwww!" The girl started to cry, her hands pressed into the dirt.

"Omigosh! Are you all right?" Natalie asked, dropping to the ground.

"I hurt my knee!" the girl cried, her face all red as she rolled over onto her backside.

Natalie winced at the cut on the girl's leg, all caked with dirt. "Oh. It's not that bad."

"It's not?" the girl asked hopefully.

Someone crouched down next to Natalie and her heart caught when she realized it was Logan himself. "Nah. Not bad at all," he said.

Natalie smiled at him and he smiled back. Just then, the girl's counselor joined them, having successfully convinced the rest of her group to stay still for five minutes.

"Lisa! What happened?" the counselor asked.

Lisa sniffled bravely. "I hurt my knee. But it's not that bad," she said, mimicking Natalie's words.

The counselor smiled gratefully at Natalie and Logan. "No. It's just tiny, actually. But we'd better take you to the nurse to get cleaned up," the counselor suggested.

"I want *her* to take me!" Lisa announced, pointing at Natalie.

Nat laughed. "Okay. I can do that." She held out her hands to the girl and hoisted her to her feet. "You okay to walk?"

"Yeah," Lisa said.

"Are you sure?" the counselor asked Natalie.

"It's no problem," Natalie replied.

"I'll go with them," Logan offered. "You know, make sure they get there okay."

Natalie's heart skipped a beat and she grinned. The counselor eyed them both suspiciously, but the girls in her group were starting to get loud and she made a snap decision.

"Okay, fine. If I don't get some food in these kids soon, they're gonna revolt, anyway. Just take her right there and bring her right to the mess hall when you're done."

"Ma'am, yes ma'am," Logan joked.

"Come on, Lisa," Natalie said, taking the girl's hand. Lisa clutched her fingers tightly. "Let's go see Nurse Helen."

A few minutes later, Lisa was getting a yellow smiley-face bandage from the nurse inside the first-aid cabin, while Natalie and Logan stood in the outer doorway, leaning back against opposite sides.

"That was really cool, the way you stopped for her," Logan said to Natalie, touching her sneaker with the toe of his. "Not everyone would have done that."

"Really?" Natalie said.

"Are you kidding? Most of the girls around here are so self-absorbed, they would have stepped right over the kid," Logan said.

Natalie blushed and smiled. "Well, why did *you* stop?"

"I got hurt my first summer here and I remember how scary it was. Even a little thing like that, when you're away from home for the first time and your mom isn't there to take care of you?" Logan shuddered. "It's no good."

*Oh my gosh. Could he be any sweeter?* Natalie thought.

"Oh, so you're a mama's boy," she joked.

"Guilty as charged," Logan shot back with a grin.

Natalie's heart pounded happily away. It was official. This was a megacrush she had going on here.

"She's all set," Nurse Helen announced, ushering Lisa back to the door. "Your friends are gonna take you back to lunch now, okay, hon?"

"Okay!" Lisa announced.

"Wanna hold my hand?" Logan asked.

Lisa rolled her eyes. "I'm eight. I'm not a baby," she said.

Natalie, Logan, and Helen all cracked up laughing as Lisa huffed by them, all brave now that she was cleaned up and bandaged.

"I like this kid!" Logan announced.

"Me too," Natalie replied.

They held each other's gaze for a long moment, and Natalie got the sense that Logan wasn't *just* talking about Lisa. He was saying that he liked *her*, too. And the feeling was definitely mutual.

▲ ▲ ▲

Tori sat on a log at the campfire that night, alone. The rest of her bunk was gathered closer to the fire, making s'mores. She saw Jenna drop her fifth marshmallow into the fire and groan in frustration. After five summers at camp, Tori would think Jenna would know how to make a s'more. But the girl liked her marshmallows burned and almost always left them in the fire too long.

Candace gave Jenna a perfectly formed s'more, then started to make another one for herself. Tori smiled at Candace's generosity. She wished she could get in on the fun, but she just was not in the mood. She couldn't stop thinking about the relay race and how badly she'd messed up. Then, every time she thought about it, she remembered that she didn't even like Color War. If it wasn't for Belle's idea of choosing captains by chance, she wouldn't even *care* about this stuff. She sighed and leaned back on her hands, pressing her palms into the cold ground. She couldn't wait until this week was over.

Suddenly a chant rose up from the other side of the fire, started by the fifth-division boys on the Red team.

*"Red team! Red team!*
*Can't be beat!*
*Blue team! Blue team!*
*Kiss our feet!"*

Everyone on the Red team cheered, and instantly the sixth-division guys on the other side of the fire added their own cheer.

*"We are Blue!*
*The mighty, mighty Blue!*
*Watch your backs, Red!*
*We're coming for you!"*

More cheers and jeers followed and soon most of the camp was caught up in the chanting. Natalie walked over from the fire and dropped down next to Tori on her log. Tori sat up and crossed her arms over her chest, pulling herself in tighter. She'd barely seen Natalie all day, and for some reason seeing her now made her feel annoyed.

"Hey! Want one?" Natalie asked, offering Tori a s'more.

"No thanks," Tori said.

"So what's up? Why so glum?"

"Remember when you said we would deal with the captain thing together?" Tori asked.

"Yeah . . ." Natalie said blankly.

"Well, I needed your help today and you weren't there," she said. "I had no idea what to do when I was picking the team and I completely messed it up."

"I'm so sorry, Tori," Natalie said. "I was all caught up in this conversation and I didn't even realize we were up until Clarissa dragged me away and told me to get down to the dock."

"Oh," Tori said. She wished Lainie had never come over to their bunk that morning. If the girl had never talked to Natalie, then Natalie would have been with Tori the whole time and none of this would have happened. Team Blue actually might have had a chance to win their first event.

"But don't worry, it was just the first day," Natalie told her. "We have *tons* of time to stage a comeback."

"Yeah?" Tori said hopefully.

"Definitely," Natalie said. "And I promise I will not steer any more kayaks onto the entirely wrong shore."

"Sorry about that," Tori said, brightening slightly. "I really had no idea you couldn't kayak."

"Well, now we *all* know," Natalie joked. "But it turned out okay, anyway, because I met this guy."

"Really?" Tori said with a grin. Suddenly Color War was completely out of her mind. There was nothing like a little gossip to make a girl feel better. Especially romantic gossip.

"Oh my gosh, he is *so* cute," Natalie gushed. "He was standing right there when—"

"Natalie! *There* you are!" Lainie Wilcox appeared out of nowhere and grabbed Natalie's hand, hoisting her up in the middle of her sentence. "I've been looking all over for you!"

*Hello, rude!* Tori thought. Apparently Grace and Alex were right. Lainie really did only care about herself. Natalie looked as shocked as Tori felt by the interruption and Tori waited for her friend to tell the girl off.

"Really?" Natalie said, blatantly excited.

Lainie laughed. "First of all, you should never act all surprised and psyched when someone says they've been looking for you. Always—"

"Always act like you were right in the middle of something important," Natalie finished. "You read *Cosmo!*"

"Of course I read *Cosmo.* What self-respecting girl doesn't?" Lainie said.

"Tori doesn't," Natalie pointed out. "She's more of a *Vogue* girl."

"That's me," Tori said halfheartedly.

"Oh, well I read *Vogue*, too, but there's nothing like *Cosmo* for real-life advice," Lainie sniffed.

*Right. Advice on how to snag guys, how to change yourself for guys, how to play games with guys. Yeehaw,* Tori thought sarcastically. Meanwhile, Natalie and Lainie whispered to each other and giggled, and Tori couldn't help wondering if whatever they'd said was about her. But no. Natalie wouldn't mock her . . . would she?

"So, did you bring it?" Lainie asked.

"Got it right here," Natalie said, patting the pocket of her sweatshirt.

"Got what?" Tori asked.

"I told Lainie and the girls I'd give them a Blue-team pedicure tonight," Natalie said. "Wanna come?"

Tori looked at Lainie, who stared back at her like she was totally undesirable. "Yeah. You should come," the girl said with zero enthusiasm.

"Thanks anyway. I think I'm going to go get some s'mores," Tori replied, getting up.

"Okay," Natalie said. She was clearly completely oblivious to the fact that Lainie didn't like Tori at all. "I'll talk to you later, Tori."

And then, off went Tori's best friend, trailing after the most obnoxious girl at Camp Lakeview.

▲ ▲ ▲

Lainie's friends sat in a circle on a flat rock just off the edge of the clearing where the campfire was held. Natalie had noticed them over here before, and it had always seemed so cool, like they had their own private space. They even had their own light source, since they were so far from the fire. Three large, standing flashlights were set up in the center of the rock, pointed in all directions.

"I think it's so cool that you even thought to bring blue nail polish to camp," Lainie said as they made their way over. "I never think that far ahead."

"I guess I'm kind of a planner," Natalie admitted.

"Not me. I'm a spur-of-the-moment girl," Lainie said. "Like this morning. I saw you doing your toes and I thought 'I have to talk to that girl. She seems cool.' So I did."

Natalie felt a rush of pride. Lainie thought she was cool! "Thanks. I'm glad you came over."

"You're welcome," Lainie said with a laugh.

Natalie's brow knit. Did that mean what she thought it meant? That Lainie thought Natalie *should* be grateful she introduced herself? Nah. No one was *that* full of themselves. Or if they were, they weren't that obvious about it. Lainie must have meant something else.

"Got her!" Lainie announced, sitting down between Daniella and Liliko in what appeared to be the only free space.

"Hey, Nat!" Trish said, as the other girls gave her vague hellos.

"Hi." Natalie stood on the edge of the circle, feeling awkward. There was no place for her to sit, so she shoved her hands into the back pockets of her denim shorts and tried to look casual. "So . . . who wants to go first?"

She pulled the nail polish out of the pocket of

her pink zip hoodie.

"Do me!" Lainie said, shoving her feet forward.

Finally, the other girls parted so that Natalie could get through the circle. She climbed into the center of the circle and sat down at Lainie's feet. It was pretty dark, what with her back blocking one of the flashlights, but she figured she had to at least try. She pulled her toe separators out of her pocket and placed them on Lainie's feet.

"Wow. You really do come prepared. Like a Boy Scout," Lainie said, a hint of teasing in her voice. Natalie let it slide and got to work. Lainie wouldn't think the toe separators were so funny when she had perfectly unsmudged nails.

"So, Lainie, any Christopher contact today?" Daniella asked as Natalie painted Lainie's big toenail.

"Totally. You all saw it!" Lainie said. Her friends stared at her blankly. "At lunch? When he asked me if he could have our salt?"

"Oh, yeah. Did you *see* the way he looked at her?" Patty said. "He's totally crushing on you, Lain."

"Oh, *totally*," Trish agreed.

"Right? I mean he could have asked any of us, but he asked me," Lainie said excitedly, sitting up slightly. Her foot jerked and Natalie painted a blue line across the side of her big toe.

"Oops. Sorry," she said.

Liliko scrounged a tissue out of her woven purse and handed it to Natalie. Natalie quickly wiped off the mistake.

"So, Christopher is . . . ?" Natalie said.

"Her lifelong crush," Daniella announced, shooing a moth away with a wave of her hand. "Only it's been six summers and they *still* haven't even smooched."

"Hello? His parents didn't allow him to date before now," Lainie said. "But I have it on good authority that he had a girlfriend during the school year, so there's no stopping me now."

"So what's he like?" Natalie asked, psyched to get some sixth-division gossip.

"Oh, he's totally cute. He has light blond hair and these amazing green eyes. He's kind of short, I'll admit, but totally athletic," Lainie replied dreamily. "Plus he's a camp legacy, like me. And every year we've been here we've been on the same team for Color War."

"It's like fate," Liliko said.

"He sounds perfect for you," Natalie put in.

"You think?" Lainie asked excitedly.

"Are you kidding? Athletic, hot, and a legacy? You guys would be, like, king and queen of the camp," Natalie said.

Lainie grinned. "I like the way you think, Goode."

Natalie's heart fluttered at the compliment. This was going very well.

"Um, that's only what we've all been saying for years," Patty interrupted. "But camp is almost over, Lain. When are you going to make your move already?"

Lainie blushed slightly at this and leaned back on her hands. Clearly she was embarrassed, and Natalie's heart went out to her. She knew how hard it could be when your friends wanted to get involved with your love life.

"Well, sometimes you've gotta be delicate with these things," Natalie said. "She can't just pounce on the guy. She might freak him out."

"Exactly!" Lainie said, her eyes brightening. "See? This girl knows what she's talking about. She totally dated that fifth-division hottie for, like, two summers. What's his name, again?"

Natalie grinned. She could not believe that Lainie had been keeping tabs on her. "Simon," she said. "But we're just friends now."

*There's another certain someone I'm interested in,* she thought, her heart fluttering. But she wasn't about to bring that up now. Not when she had no idea whether that certain someone was interested in her.

"You stayed friends?" Trish said in awe. "Wow. That's, like, impossible."

"Yeah. What did you do, hypnotize the guy?" Liliko joked.

"The girl's good," Lainie said with a smile. "Bet you could all take some pointers from her."

Natalie saw Daniella and Patty exchange an irritated glance, but she ignored them. She didn't much care what the two loudmouths thought of her. All that mattered were Lainie and the other *nice* girls.

"Do me next!" Trish exclaimed as Natalie finished up Lainie's toes.

"No problem," Natalie said, scooting over.

And clearly, when it came to Lainie, Trish, and Liliko, Natalie was totally in.

chapter

# FIVE

"Score!"

Tori gasped for breath as Jenna slammed the soccer ball right into the back of the net. Gaby made a great dive for it, but it soared right by her outstretched fingers.

"That's three to nothing!" one of the sixth-division girls on the Red team taunted Tori. "Good luck coming back from that."

Tori felt like reaching out her foot and tripping the girl, but she couldn't. That would rank as *serious* unsportsmanlike behavior. And besides, she had to go to the center of the field for the dropping of the ball. Or whatever it was called.

"Tori! Get your head in the game!" Daniella shouted from the sidelines. She and her little friend Patty had spent the entire game sitting on the bench sunning themselves. Apparently soccer was "not their thing." Well, it wasn't Tori's either, but at least she was trying.

Clarissa, who was acting as one of the referees, dropped the ball, and Alex and Jenna both lunged for it. Jenna got control and kicked it upfield to Priya. Once again, Tori found herself running toward her own goal, just hoping to stop the ball somehow before Red scored. For a *fourth* time.

Then Tori saw Alex sprinting up behind Priya.

"Go! Go! Go!" Tori shouted, running as fast as she could in case someone needed to pass to her.

Alex deftly stole the ball and turned around, moving right back in the other direction.

"Yes!" Tori cried, almost tripping herself as she turned on her heel.

"Go, Alex! Go!" Lainie shouted.

Tori raced upfield. There was no one in front of her. Maybe Alex would pass her the ball. Maybe she could actually *score!* She saw herself booting the ball with the side of her foot. Saw it sailing over the head of the sixth-division girl in front of the net and saw her entire team crowding around her in glee. The very idea made Tori giddy. What she wouldn't give to do *something* right in this Color War.

"Tori! Hold up!" someone shouted from the sidelines.

The whistle blew and suddenly Clarissa was standing right in front of her. "Offside!" she cried, waving her arm.

"What?" Tori asked, stopping short. Her lungs hurt from all the running and she put her hands on her hips.

"Sorry, Tori. You were offside," Clarissa said with a shrug. "Red gets the ball."

*Offside?* Tori thought. *What in the world is offside?* "Huh? But I don't—"

"Oh, man!" Gaby shouted from the goal.

"What are you *doing?*" Liliko yelled from somewhere behind her.

"Even *I* know that," Daniella said.

"Can I get a time out?" Lainie shouted, throwing her hands up in a T. She looked exasperated as she trudged to the sidelines.

"That's a time out, Blue team!" Clarissa shouted, blowing her whistle again.

Tori, along with the rest of her exhausted team, followed after Lainie. Now that Tori had stopped running around, she could feel all of her muscles tightening and the icky feeling of her shirt sticking to her body. Why anybody *wanted* to do sports was beyond her.

"All right, that's it," Lainie said, grabbing a paper cup full of water. "Tori, Candace, Natalie—you guys are out. Daniella, Patty, Trish, you're in."

"Wait a minute! You can't do that!" Tori protested.

"Oh, I think I just did," Lainie snapped in reply. "There's no way we're gonna win this thing with a bunch of girls on the field who don't even know the rules."

"That is so not fair. They don't even *want* to play!" Tori replied, venting her frustration. "Besides, you can't just decide for all of us. I'm a captain, too, you know."

Lainie snorted a laugh. "Yeah, but you're fifth division and I'm sixth, which means I overrule you. Besides, you clearly have no idea what you're doing."

"Hey!" Alex cried.

"Uh, isn't that a little bit harsh?" Gaby piped in.

Tori felt buoyed by her friends sticking up for her, but she couldn't help noticing that Natalie wasn't saying a thing. What had happened to "we're in this together?" It was almost like Natalie was taking Lainie's side. Like maybe Nat's friendship with Lainie was more important to her than her friendship with Tori. On top of all the gasping for breath and the muscle pain, now Tori's heart hurt, too.

"I'm just trying to win Color War," Lainie said, crushing her cup and tossing it toward a nearby garbage can. It fell right in, of course. "Isn't that what we *all* want to do?"

"Yeah," a few of the girls mumbled halfheartedly.

"That was lame. Do you want to win or not?" Lainie shouted.

"Yeah!" everyone, even Natalie, shouted in return. Tori felt like she was going to burst into humiliated tears.

"Then let's get out there and do it!"

The team clapped and cheered as they ran back onto the field, but Tori felt completely deflated. She dropped onto the bench and hung her head. Candace sat down next to her and placed her hand gently on Tori's shoulder. Tori appreciated the effort and tried to smile, but it was difficult.

"Well, she does have a point," Natalie said, sitting as well. "The three of us *don't* have any clue what we're doing out there."

It was so the last thing Tori wanted to hear. She didn't even acknowledge what Natalie said, and didn't look up when Natalie stood again and started roaming the sidelines, cheering for their team. She also didn't look up when the Blue team scored a goal, then another, then another. Not even when Lainie made the final goal right before the buzzer, bringing the Blue team a victory.

▲ ▲ ▲

"That was an amazing goal you made, Lainie," Natalie gushed that evening on the way to dinner. "It was, like, right out of the Olympics or something."

"I just did what I had to do to win," Lainie said modestly, lifting her shoulders.

"I wish I could have helped, but soccer is *not* my thing," Natalie said. There was total silence. No one disagreed with her. Natalie felt a twinge of embarrassment in her stomach. She felt like they were all laughing behind her back.

"Yeah, but you cheered for us on the sidelines," Lainie said finally. "That totally helped."

"Yeah?" Natalie asked uncertainly.

"Definitely. Right, guys?" Lainie looked around at her friends and they all chorused their agreement. "See? Cheering the team on is just as important as being out on the field," Lainie said, patting Natalie on the back.

"Thanks," Natalie said, buoyed. "I *can* be very loud."

Lainie and the other girls chuckled.

"Oh, hey! There's Tori! I'll be right back," Natalie said.

She jogged up ahead, dodging a couple of younger boys who were waging a thumb-wrestling match as they walked, and came up alongside Tori and Candace.

"Hey, guys!" Natalie said. "How's it going?"

Tori stared straight ahead as she walked. "Fine."

Natalie's chest tightened. Was Tori purposely being cold to her? "What's wrong?" she asked.

"Nothing," Tori said.

"Wait, are you still mad about the soccer game?" Natalie asked. "So Lainie took us out. We never would have won if the three of us had stayed in. What's the big deal?"

Tori stopped walking and turned to Natalie, her sandals crunching on the rocky path. "She totally humiliated me!" Tori cried, her eyes wet. "She basically told me I stunk right in front of everyone! And what was with that overruling thing? No one ever said that older captains could overrule younger ones."

"Tori, I . . . I'm sorry if your feelings were hurt, but she did turn out to be kind of right, didn't she?" Natalie said, biting her lip.

Tori's jaw dropped and she made a high-pitched noise. An offended noise.

"What? I mean, we *did* win with the team she chose," Natalie said. "And the rest of us can participate in other stuff. *Someone* had to sit on the sidelines."

"I have to go," Tori said flatly.

Then she turned around and speed-walked off, her arms crossed tightly over her stomach.

"Me too," Candace said. Then she raced off after Tori.

Natalie stood there, letting the rest of the crowd go around her. What was wrong with Tori? Natalie thought she hadn't even wanted to be captain, so why was she taking the whole thing so seriously?

She took a deep breath and looked around. Maybe she should find Alex or Belle or someone and try to figure this out. But instead, her eyes met someone else's. They met Logan's intense blue eyes. He was looking at her from all the way on the far side of the still moving crowd. Natalie's heart skipped a couple dozen beats and she smiled.

"*Hey*," Logan mouthed, lifting his hand in a wave.

"*Hey*," Natalie replied, waving as well.

And just like that, Tori and her weird overreacting were all but forgotten.

Priya walked into the newspaper cabin for her first elective session, just hoping it would go by quickly. It was so difficult, trying to concentrate on normal camp things when Color War was going on. But Dr. Steve insisted the camp maintain *some* sense of schedule, so mornings were still the same as always—elective classes each day. Then in the afternoon, the competition would erupt all over again. Priya's nerves sizzled just thinking about it.

Inside the newspaper office, a dozen kids of all ages milled about, flipping through old issues or looking at photos on a lightboard, waiting for the counselor to start the session. At first, everyone was just a murky shadow, but as soon as her eyes adjusted from the bright sunlight to the dimmer fluorescents, Priya noticed that Tori was sitting at a table near the center of the room.

And she was chewing on her hair.

"Hey, Tori!" Priya said with a grin, pulling up a stool. "I didn't know you were in newspaper!"

Tori dropped her long blond ponytail and swung it over her shoulder. "Yep. I was hoping to do a gossip column or a fashion piece, but Dana already negged them both," she said with a sigh.

Dana was the counselor in charge of the newspaper, and she took her job very seriously. Rumor had it she was off to Harvard in the fall and was hoping to get a job on the Ivy League school's esteemed paper. She was a *real* reporter, so the Camp Lakeview newspaper had to be a *real* paper.

"Well, I'm sure you'll think of something else to do," Priya said confidently, pulling last week's issue of the newspaper from the center of the table. "Hey! Maybe we can do something together!"

Tori smiled wryly. "You sure that would be okay? Red team and Blue team on the same side?"

"There's no Color War in here, right?" Priya said. "At least, that's what Dr. Steve says."

"Thank God," Tori replied, rolling her eyes. She slumped forward slightly and toyed with a wax pencil on the table.

"Hey, is everything okay?" Priya asked.

"No. Not really," Tori replied. She looked up, her eyebrows raised. "How do you do it? How are you such a good captain?"

Priya laughed—until she realized Tori was not laughing with her. "You're serious?"

"Dead," Tori said, turning fully on her stool to

face her. "I'm so bad at all these events. I must be the worst captain ever."

*Wow. She must really be desperate if she's asking the enemy for help,* Priya thought. Part of her felt like she shouldn't be giving Tori any pointers. They were, after all, on opposite sides. Jenna would throttle her if she knew that Priya was even *thinking* about helping the Blue team. But Priya was a good friend first, a Color War obsessive second.

"Being a good captain isn't about being good at all the events," Priya said, keeping her voice down. "It's about motivation. All you've got to do is give them one good pep talk and they'll get behind you."

"Yeah?" Tori asked hopefully.

"Yeah. Victory is ninety-nine percent attitude," Priya said. "Just ask Seabiscuit."

Tori laughed. It was the first real smile Priya had seen on the girl's face in days.

"Where do you get all this stuff?" Tori asked.

"My basketball coach back home is a real character," Priya said. "She's got all kinds of great catchphrases."

"Well, thanks," Tori said, sitting up straight. "I really appreciate it."

"Just don't tell Jenna I helped you," Priya told her. "I don't want to wake up with a frog in my cot or something."

Tori grinned. "I promise."

chapter

# SIX

When Tori walked out of the mess hall after lunch, a stage was set up in the clearing just outside the building. It hadn't been there when she'd gone in, but there it stood, as if it had magically appeared from nowhere. It was a wooden structure with a big banner strung over it. The banner, much to Tori's dread, read: PIE-EATING CONTEST!

Dr. Steve stepped up behind the table that stood in the center of the stage and lifted his megaphone. "Welcome, campers, to this year's super-colossal pie-eating contest!"

"Woo-hoo! Yeah! This is *so* my event!" Jenna shouted, skipping through the crowd.

"Like everyone doesn't already know that," Gaby said under her breath.

Tori turned around and looked at her team. This was just what she needed. An event they were *guaranteed* to lose. No one could out-eat Jenna. Especially not after a lunch of hot dogs, potato chips, and bug juice.

"Can I please have the first-division boys

and girls come to the front?" Dr. Steve shouted.

*Okay, at least I have a little time before they get to our division,* Tori thought. She looked around and spotted a tall elm tree near the side of the mess hall.

"Come on, you guys," she said, taking Candace's hand.

"Where're we going?" Grace asked.

"We need a sit-down," Tori said, throwing out some Hollywood speak.

The team followed her over to the tree, where Tori dropped to the ground. Everyone was watching her intently. That, at least, was a good start. This was her team. All she had to do was motivate them. Alex, Grace, Gaby, Candace, and . . .

"Where's Natalie?" Tori asked.

"Where is she ever?" Gaby said, gesturing over her shoulder.

Tori looked up and, sure enough, Natalie was hanging out toward the back of the crowd with Lainie and her friends, laughing and pointing as the little kids onstage tried to eat their way through the pudding-and-whipped-cream pies. Tori felt her heart turn to stone just watching Natalie and Lainie act all buddy-buddy. Apparently Natalie really had forgotten her promise to help Tori out with the Color War captainship. Well, fine. If that was the kind of friend she wanted to be, then Tori would just ignore her right back.

"Should I go get her?" Alex said, already half up.

"No. Forget it," Tori said flatly. "Let's just do this. All right. Who's going to be our representative in the pie eating?"

All the girls looked at one another. No one said a word.

"Come on, you guys, *somebody* has to go up there," Tori said. The entire camp erupted in cheers. Someone had just won up onstage, and the second division kids were up.

"Not me," Gaby said, leaning back on her hands. "There's no way I'm going up against Jenna Bloom. It's totally pointless."

"It *is* totally pointless," Candace agreed.

"Yeah. Whoever goes up there is gonna lose," Grace put in. "*And* get all gross trying."

Tori sighed. "Look, you guys. I know Jenna's good, but she's not unbeatable." Tori knew it was a lie even as the words were coming out of her mouth, but that was what pep talks were all about, wasn't it?

"Yeah she is!" Gaby said, eyes wide.

"Please?" Tori tried. "Somebody has to do it. Alex?"

"I would. I really would," Alex said. "But I can't eat that much sugar that fast. It's bad for my health."

If anyone else had said this, Tori might have laughed them off, but with Alex it was true. She had diabetes and had to be very careful about her sugar intake.

"Right. I forgot. I'm sorry." Okay, the pep talk thing clearly wasn't working. What else could she do to motivate her team? Tori wracked her brain and an idea suddenly popped into her mind. Her father was an entertainment lawyer and he dealt with stars' contracts all the time. And what did those contracts build in for incentive? Perks!

"What if I gave you unlimited use of all my makeup and beauty supplies for the whole rest of the summer?" Tori suggested, looking around at Gaby, Grace, and Candace.

"What, are you bribing us now?" Gaby said, clearly disgusted.

"I don't think you can do that," Grace put in.

Tori's face heated up and she felt completely foolish. She *was* trying to bribe them. She was trying to *bribe* her Color War team. How desperate could she get?

"Tori! There you are!" Clarissa came jogging over in her blue T-shirt. "They need to know who's gonna represent your team."

Tori's heart started to pound. She looked from one face to the next. Alex shrugged, Gaby scowled, Grace looked up in the sky and whistled, Candace went white as a ghost. Tori swallowed hard, realizing what she was going to have to do.

"I guess I am."

She pushed herself shakily to her feet and no one tried to stop her.

"Good luck," Grace said weakly.

*I'll need it,* Tori thought sourly.

Ten minutes later, Tori found herself up onstage along with Jenna. Adam Bloom was up there as well, representing the Blue team fifth-division boys, while Jenna's boyfriend, David, was representing the Red team for the boys. With these three eating next to her, Tori was going to come in dead last.

"You're going up against me?" Jenna said, slapping her knee. "No offense, Tori, but you couldn't eat one pretzel faster than me. Good luck! You're *so* going to need it!"

Tori suddenly felt sick to her stomach. It wasn't like she didn't expect Jenna to trash talk her. The girl lived for this stuff. But it was one more moment of humiliation to pile on top of all the others.

*Why am I doing this?* Tori wondered. *I've totally lost my mind.*

Pete, the camp's cook, walked up and placed the pies down on the table. Tori looked down at the metal tin full off graham cracker crust, chocolate pudding, whipped cream, and gummy worms. The very idea of eating all that sugar and fat made her gag.

"All right, everyone! Take your seats!" Dr. Steve announced.

Tori moved toward her chair. She glanced out at the crowd, looking for Natalie, hoping to at least get a thumbs-up or a smile of support. But when she found Nat in the crowd, the girl was so wrapped up in conversation with Lainie, she didn't even seem to realize Tori was competing.

"The key is to not chew. Just swallow," Adam said as he sat down next to her.

Tori's stomach turned.

"On your mark! Get set! Go!"

And the next thing she knew, Tori's carefully made-up face was in the pie.

"Omigod. You could not pay me to do this," Lainie said, turning away from the pie-eating contest. "Eating a whole pie without your hands? That is so unsanitary."

"I know. It's pretty gross. And it's not like it's a camp skill," Natalie said.

"Exactly!" Lainie replied. "You know, Nat, sometimes it's like we share the same brain. I wish you were in sixth division so we could hang out more."

"Me too." Natalie grinned happily. "Okay, but what if someone gave you a thousand dollars? Would you do it then?"

"No way," Lainie replied.

"Well, what *would* you eat for a thousand dollars?" Natalie asked.

"Hmmm . . . interesting," Lainie said. "Without hands, or with?"

"Without," Natalie said.

"Nothing. No eating without hands in public," Lainie said. "I mean, what are we, pigs? Look at those people."

Natalie stood on her toes, trying to see over the crowd and figure out who was up on the stage. Unfortunately, they were all facedown in their pies and it was impossible to tell any of the competitors apart.

"Okay, you have a point," Natalie said. "But if I could get a thousand dollars to do whatever I wanted with, I would eat . . . an entire banana split with no hands."

"Please. You'd totally get brain freeze," Lainie said, rolling her eyes like she was so much older and wiser.

"Good point," Natalie said.

"Okay, new topic." Lainie twirled her hair around her finger. "How do I get Christopher to notice me?"

"I don't understand. I thought the other girls said he was crushing on you," Natalie said, forgetting about pies for the moment.

"That's their opinion," Lainie said. "And sometimes . . . the way he looks at me . . . I think they might be right. But other times I'm not so sure."

Natalie shook her head. "Boys. They should really come with a user's manual."

Lainie laughed. "Seriously."

Natalie beamed. "Okay, you have talked to him before, though, right?"

"Here and there," Lainie said, lifting her shoulder. "But it's always about sports or camp or Color War. Sometimes I think he just thinks of me as one of the guys."

Natalie looked Lainie up and down. She was tall, had perfect legs and gorgeous hair, and the longest eyelashes Natalie had ever seen. "If he thinks that, he's a moron and you shouldn't date him, anyway," Natalie joked.

"I'm serious here!" Lainie said, bouncing up and down. "You always look so perfect. What should I do? Do you think I need to be more girly? Maybe I could do something with my hair . . ."

"Lainie, you don't have to do anything," Natalie told her. "You're already the prettiest girl in camp."

"Please," Lainie said with a scoff, looking down at her sneakers.

"You are! Everyone knows it!"

"Well, Christopher doesn't," Lainie said, screwing her mouth up into a scowl.

Natalie stared at Lainie for a long moment. This girl had a serious self-confidence problem. How was that even possible when she walked around camp like she owned the place?

*Guess everyone has their secrets,* Natalie thought. And here was Lainie Wilcox, Queen of Camp Lakeview, sharing her secrets with Natalie.

"Okay, how about this—the next time we have a free period, I'll help you pick out an outfit," Natalie said. "Something fabulous that's still totally you."

"Yes!" Lainie squealed, hugging Natalie quickly. "I was so hoping you'd say that!"

"That's what friends are for, right?" Natalie said with a grin.

"Winner! Jenna Bloom!" Dr. Steve announced into the megaphone.

Natalie looked up, surprised. She hadn't even realized that was *her* division up there already. Jenna thrust her arms in the air, her face covered with chocolate, and bits of whipped cream stuck to her curly hair. Natalie got up on her toes, wondering who had represented the Blue team.

In the next second, she got her answer. Tori jumped up from the table, hand over her mouth, looking waxy and pale. She ran down the steps and into the woods just outside the mess hall. A concerned murmur raced through the crowd and everyone fell silent. Two seconds later, all anyone could hear were the sounds of

Tori throwing up. A lot.

"Ugh!" everyone groaned.

"Oh my God!" Natalie cried. How embarrassing. Poor Tori! She had to find out if she was okay. But Natalie had only taken one step when Lainie grabbed her hand.

"Okay, the new me," Lainie said, her eyes bright with excitement. "Where do we start?"

"I . . . uh . . ."

Nat looked over her shoulder and saw Belle and Clarissa hustling over to help Tori. Part of her really wanted to go over there, but maybe it would be better if Tori wasn't surrounded by people right now. She probably felt awful enough as it was, without having it shoved in her face that everyone had seen and heard her puking.

Natalie focused on Lainie and tried to smile. "Well, like I said, I guess we should start with clothes . . ."

▲ ▲ ▲

"Are you feeling any better?" Nurse Carrie asked Tori, who was propped up on about eight pillows on a cot in the infirmary.

"A little."

Tori took the cup of water the nurse was offering and sipped at it. Carrie was the new nurse's aide this year—young and thin, with dark hair that was always back in a bun. She probably would have been beautiful if she ever wore any makeup or put on something cuter than the big pajama-style scrubs she was always wearing. It was like the woman was pretending she was in the cast of *ER*.

"You know, I threw up in front of an entire wedding once," Carrie said, pulling up a chair.

"You did?" Tori asked.

"Oh, yeah, but unlike you I didn't even have a tree to hide behind," Carrie said. "It was last summer, and it was my sister's wedding. The night before, we all went out for seafood because it's her favorite, and I woke up feeling not quite right. I figured it might be food poisoning, but I was the maid of honor, so it wasn't like I could stay home sick. So I just had some crackers and tried to ignore it. But then I got into my bridesmaid's dress and it was *so* tight. And the church was, like, a million degrees. And all of a sudden, just as my sister was about to say 'I do,' I felt it happening."

"What did you do?" Tori asked, sitting forward.

"Let's just say I had to buy the pastor a new pair of shoes," Carrie said, cringing.

Tori laughed and so did Carrie. "See? You'll be able to laugh about this one day."

Tori's heart turned as she remembered the grossed-out sounds coming from the other campers as she crouched behind that tree. "I don't think so."

"Believe me, last summer I *never* would have thought I could laugh about that, but here I am." She lifted her hands as she stood, and Tori smiled weakly. Actually, Carrie *was* pretty, with or without makeup and cool clothes. "So, your counselor and a bunch of your bunkmates want to see you. Should I let them in?"

Instantly, Tori wondered if Natalie was out

there, or if she was off with Lainie somewhere. Either option didn't appeal much. If Natalie *wasn't* out there, that meant she really didn't care about Tori anymore. But if she *was* out there, she was pretty much the last person Tori wanted to deal with just then. She couldn't take pity from Natalie on top of everything else.

"Actually, could I just see Belle first?" Tori asked.

"Sure," Carrie said.

She walked out of the recovery room and, seconds later, a very concerned-looking Belle came in. Tori sat up and swung her legs over the side of the bed as Belle perched on Carrie's vacated chair. Tori knew what she had to do. It was all she'd been thinking about since the moment she realized she was going to lose her lunch *and* the entire pie. But her pulse raced with nervousness nevertheless.

"Are you okay?" Belle asked, her dark eyes searching Tori's face. "I told them the pie-eating contest could only be trouble, but do they listen to first-year counselors? Nooo."

"I'm fine," Tori said firmly. "But I don't want to be captain anymore, Belle. I quit."

The moment the words were out of her mouth, Tori felt ten times lighter. She should have done this on day one.

"I don't think you really want to do that," Belle said.

"Yes, I do," Tori said.

"But what will your team think?" Belle asked.

"They'll probably be relieved!" Tori told her. "I

haven't done a single thing right."

"That's not true!" Belle said automatically.

"Fine. Name one thing," Tori challenged, lifting her chin.

Belle looked at her blankly. "Well, I . . . you . . ."

Tori felt her spirits sink slightly. She really *hadn't* done anything right.

"You can't quit," Belle said finally. "I won't let you."

Desperation welled up in Tori's chest like a water balloon. "Belle—"

"No, Tori. If you quit now, you're going to regret it, I swear. Part of my job is to help you guys deal with stuff like this, and as far as I'm concerned, quitting is not the way to handle a tough situation." Belle stood up and started pacing in front of Tori, between the two beds. "I know you didn't ask to be captain, but your team is counting on you now. You can't let them down."

"But that's all I've done," Tori said.

"If you really think that, then you should try to turn it around," Belle told her. "You can do this, Tori. I know you can. All you've got to do is play to your strengths."

"I don't have any strengths!" Tori cried. "I stink at everything camp. I don't even know what I'm doing here right now!"

"Tori—"

"No. Forget it," Tori said, jumping up. "If you won't listen to me, then I'm just going back to the bunk."

She turned and ran out of the recovery room,

nearly slamming right into Priya in the doorway. Priya took a step back, her mouth hanging open slightly. Tori's eyes met hers, and in that one second she knew that Priya had overheard it all. She knew what a loser Tori was. Such a loser that she couldn't even convince Belle to let her quit.

"Hey. I . . . I was just coming to see if you were okay," Priya said.

"Thanks," Tori replied. "I have to go."

Then she ran out of the infirmary as fast as she possibly could.

▲ ▲ ▲

Dear Michael,

Okay, forget all about my last letter. I do _not_ belong at camp. You're never going to believe what happened the day after I wrote to you. Color War started. Okay, that's not a shocker, but the shocker was, I was made captain of the fifth-division Blue team. It was totally by chance that I got it. It _had_ to be by chance. These girls _never_ would have _elected_ me captain. Why?

# BECAUSE I STINK AT BEING A CAPTAIN!

Ugh! I can't get anything right, and I hate it. I feel frustrated basically all the time. And the most annoying thing about it is that I don't even care about Color War. I didn't care about it last year and I wasn't supposed to care about it this year, either. But now I have to. I have to care about it a lot. Because I'm the captain and my friends are counting on me. They, by the way, care about Color War more than anything. Honestly. I think they care about it more than school and their families.

Well, that's an exaggeration. Unless you count Jenna Bloom. Thank goodness she's on the Red team. If she was on Blue, she might have murdered my useless self by now.

The point is, I don't want to let my friends down, but it seems like that's all I do.

Meanwhile, Natalie has totally been letting me down. She was supposed to be helping me with all this stuff, but instead she's been following this sixth-division girl, Lainie Wilcox, around like a puppy dog. I thought Natalie was above that kind of worshipping behavior, but apparently not. Apparently she forgets who her real friends are and about the promises she made to them the second an older girl starts paying attention to her. I mean, I know it's fun to hang out with new and potentially cool people, but I feel like I haven't really talked to her in days. And I could really use a good talk.

Can I get that hug now?


Miss you.
Tori

chapter
# SEVEN

Natalie inched forward on the line for the high dive, shivering in her already-wet bathing suit. She couldn't believe that just a few years ago she had been scared to even go up there. Now she loved the swooping feeling of taking that step off the diving board. Of letting go and waiting for the splash and the cool water to envelop her. She loved it more than almost any other feeling.

"Hey, kayak girl."

Natalie's heart caught and a hundred little butterflies beat at her chest with their wings. Okay, that feeling wasn't bad either. She was already blushing when she turned around to face Logan.

"Hey, yourself," she replied. He was wearing a cool red and orange bathing suit, and still had that medallion around his neck. "But could you not call me that? I'm trying to forget the whole thing."

Logan grinned and Natalie's heart flip-flopped. "No problem. But then I have to come up with another nickname for you."

The line inched forward. "Why can't you just use my regular name?"

"That's so predictable. I don't like to be predictable," Logan said. He touched his fingertips to his chin and thought. "Let's see, I bet a lot of people call you Nat, so that's out. Natalie, Natalie, Natalie . . ."

Every time he said her name, her skin tingled a bit more.

"How about Lee? Does anyone call you Lee?" he asked.

"Like the last part of my name? No," Natalie replied.

"Cool. Then that's it. From now on, you're Lee to me," Logan said.

Natalie was no longer shivering. Logan had his very own nickname for her. That was so incredible. It was almost like something a boyfriend would have for his girlfriend.

"I like it," Natalie said, smiling.

"Me too." Logan smiled back. "You're up, Lee," he added, lifting his chin at the diving board.

Natalie turned and saw that there was a huge space between her and the diving board. Apparently the line had continued to move without her while she was entranced by Logan. Feeling silly, she grabbed the safety railings and started up the steps, her wet feet thwapping on the plastic stairs. All the while, her heart pounded in her chest, knowing Logan was down below, watching her.

*This is serious*, Natalie thought as she stepped out onto the diving board. *I have a very serious crush.* She hadn't felt this way since she and Simon had first met. She felt like she was about to burst.

Natalie could see all the way across the lake from atop the high dive, and she spotted Tori and Candace hanging out in inner tubes in the deep section. Suddenly she knew what she was going to do.

"Go for it, Lee!" Logan shouted.

Natalie held her breath and jumped. Her feet slammed into the cold water and she immediately started to swim toward the deep section, laughing as she surfaced. She could not *wait* to share her news about Logan with Tori.

"Hey, guys!" Natalie said, getting her breathing under control as she reached Tori's tube. She grabbed the handle on the side and hung on. "You're never going to believe what just happened!"

"Oh, what?" Tori said flatly. "You talked to Lainie? Lainie asked you to braid her hair? Lainie laughed at me and you laughed right along with her?"

"Whoa," Natalie said, taken aback. This was not the response she was looking for. "What's the matter? You can't *still* be mad at Lainie about the soccer game."

"No. Not mad," Tori said with a shrug. "Not mad at Lainie, anyway." She pushed herself off her tube and started to swim away.

"Tori!" Natalie called after her, struggling with the now weightless tube. Tori ignored her and kept swimming. "What's wrong with her?" Natalie said to Candace.

"I don't know," Candace said, looking uncomfortable. "But maybe it's because, um, we all went to visit Tori yesterday after, you know, what happened. But you weren't, um, there?"

Natalie's heart sunk a touch. She had been talking to Lainie at the time, going over her outfit for wowing Christopher. "Yeah, but I heard she didn't even want to talk to anyone."

"But still, you're her best friend here, right?" Candace said, biting her lip. "Maybe she would have, um, like, talked to you?"

Natalie stared at Candace. She wasn't sure she had ever heard the girl put so many of her own thoughts in order like that.

"I should go see if she's okay," Candace said.

Then she paddled around in her inner tube and took off.

Feeling suddenly heavy, Natalie lifted Tori's vacated tube over her head, clung to the inside straps, and ducked down so that no one at water level could see her. Beneath the surface, her legs dog-paddled away, but up above, she was still. Okay, so Candace had a point. Natalie was supposed to be Tori's best friend and she hadn't been there for her right after the vomit incident. But still, Tori should have at least stuck around to talk about it. If she had done that, then Natalie would have been able to apologize and still share her news about Logan. Now Natalie's supposed BFF didn't even know what was up with Natalie's potential BF.

And what was the big deal about Lainie, anyway? So Natalie was trying to meet some new people. Was that so wrong? If anything, Tori should be trying to get along with Nat's new group, but it seemed like Tori was determined not to like them.

Call Natalie crazy, but she didn't think she was the only one who was being a lousy friend around here.

▲ ▲ ▲

"Thanks for coming to this meeting on such short notice," Priya said, looking around at the other members of the Red team. Chelsea was sitting back on her elbows with her legs splayed out in the sand. Brynn was busy combing her wet hair back off her face, while Valerie shielded herself from the spray of water coming off the comb. Alyssa sat quietly, looking serious, almost like she knew what Priya wanted to talk about, while Jenna's knee bounced up and down like mad.

"Yeah, yeah, let's get on with it already," Jenna said, looking past Priya to the lake. Her eyes trained in on some of the fifth-division boys, who were horsing around in the deep section. "Free swim is shortened thanks to Color War, and I want to get back in the lake so I can play *Jaws* on Adam and David."

"Right, okay," Priya said, taking a deep breath. She glanced around to make sure that neither Belle nor any of the other counselors were around, then lowered her voice. "I've been thinking . . . maybe we should try to lose one of the Color War events."

"What!?" Jenna screeched. "Are you insane? Have you completely and totally gone bezerko bonkerolies?"

"Bezerko bonkerolies?" Brynn asked, laughing.

"I make up words when I'm about to have a heart

attack, okay?" Jenna cried. "We can not throw—"

"Jenna!" Priya hissed, slapping her hand over her friend's mouth. "Keep it down!"

Jenna huffed and rolled her eyes, and only then did Priya remove her hand. The last thing she needed was Jenna's big lungs letting the entire camp in on her plan. This was something that Priya could probably get in big trouble for.

"We can*not* throw an event," Jenna whispered intensely. "That goes against the whole point of Color War."

"She's right," Chelsea said. "No way, no how."

"Wait a minute, you guys," Alyssa said, holding up her hands. "Let's hear what she has to say, first. Priya, why do you think we should throw an event?"

Priya smiled slightly, grateful for the ever-fair and levelheaded Alyssa. "Well, it's just . . . I kind of feel bad for Tori," Priya said, keeping her voice low. "I think she's having a really hard time—"

"Good!" Jenna blurted.

"Jenna!" Valerie scolded, clearly shocked. "Tori is your friend!"

"Not this week, she's not," Jenna grumbled, crossing her arms over her chest.

"Okay, for those of us who are not crazy and still think of Tori as our friend, I think it would really help her to win something," Priya said. "It would boost her confidence. I hate seeing her so depressed all the time."

"So you're saying we should let Blue win so Tori won't feel like such a loser," Chelsea announced.

"I wouldn't put it that way, but yeah," Priya said.
"I—"

"What!?"

Priya's heart hit her throat. Everyone froze and the girls facing Priya in the circle went white. *Please don't let that be Tori! Please don't let that be Tori!*

Slowly, Priya turned around to find Tori standing a few feet behind her, a towel wrapped around her wet bathing suit. She'd clearly just come out of the water and been on her way over here to hang out with the rest of the bunk. Instead, she'd overheard the rest of the bunk talking about her.

"Tori—"

"You guys think I'm a loser?" Tori said. "You think I'm so lame I can't even win one Color War event on my own?"

Priya's mouth felt dry, like she had gulped up a mouthful of Camp Lakeview sand. "I didn't mean—"

"Thanks a lot, you guys," Tori said, interrupting. She grabbed her bag and flip-flops and shot them a scathing look before she headed for the pathway back to the bunks. "Thanks for being such great friends."

▲ ▲ ▲

*Maybe I'll just pretend I'm sick,* Tori thought, staring into space at dinner that night as the entire world chatted happily around her. Dishes clinked, voices bounced off the high ceiling of the mess hall, laughter popped up at random all over the room. Meanwhile, all Tori could think about was getting into her bunk and pulling the covers over her head. *Maybe I could just not get out of bed all day tomorrow. Then it'll be one day closer to the closing ceremonies of Color War . . .*

She still couldn't believe that Priya was planning on throwing an event just so that Tori could win one. Who did that girl think she was?

"You know, I gotta say, Natalie really is going where no fifth-division girl has gone before," Grace said, gnawing on a dinner roll. Natalie was sitting at the next table with all the sixth-division girls, having inhaled her dinner so fast she could have been a vacuum. "I've never seen sixth-division girls even *talk* to younger campers, let alone invite them to hang out at dinner."

"Well, what Queen Lainie wants, Queen Lainie gets," Gaby said, batting her eyelashes comically.

"It's kind of lame, I think," Alex said. "I mean, if Natalie wants to make new friends, great. She can have as many friends as she wants. But I feel like I've barely seen her lately."

"Yeah, we've barely seen her," Candace put in. "And she's supposed to be on our team."

"You said it, girlfriend," Gaby said, which made Candace beam with pleasure. Hardly anyone ever agreed with Candace, because she was usually so busy agreeing with everyone else.

"She hasn't been much of a team player," Alex said, sounding resigned. "Maybe someone should talk to her."

Suddenly, Tori felt the rest of the Blue team looking at her expectantly. She sat up straight and cleared her throat. "I don't know. I think if we talk to her, she's just gonna get all defensive and tell us that we're wrong.

We have to wait for her to figure it out on her own."

"But what if she doesn't?" Grace asked, wide-eyed.

"Yeah. What if she doesn't?" Candace asked as well.

Tori slumped again. She didn't really have an answer for that. Just then, Priya pushed her chair out from the other end of the table. She walked over and leaned on the back of Natalie's empty chair, across the table from Tori. Tori's face overheated and she looked away. There was no way she was talking to Priya.

"Tori?" Priya said.

Tori kept staring stone-facedly away. All the other girls at the table were suddenly on alert. The Red team had been there for Tori's meltdown, and the Blue team could clearly sense that something was not right. Tori wished they would all just go back to their dinner. Now she felt so conspicuous, she wanted to duck under the table and disappear.

"Tori, I just wanted to say I'm sorry," Priya said, her voice pleading. "I wasn't trying to be mean. I was just trying to figure out a way to help you get your confidence back."

"What's going on?" Grace asked, curious as ever.

"She didn't tell you?" Priya asked.

"Priya wanted us to throw a Color War event," Jenna loud-whispered. "As if!"

There was a collective gasp from the Blue team. Now Tori really did sink down. Where was a good sink-hole when she needed one?

"Throw an event!? Why would you do that?"

Alex demanded.

Out of the corner of her eye, Tori could see Priya squirming. "Well, I just, I wanted to make her feel better—"

"She feels fine!" Chelsea said. "Don't you, Tori?"

"Yeah she does! Tori's a great captain," Alex added, slinging her arm around Tori's back.

"The best!" Candace put in.

Tori looked around at her friends, surprised. Suddenly she felt a bit lighter than she had just moments before.

"We just haven't peaked yet, that's all," Gaby said. "But you just wait. Sooner or later, you Reds are going down."

"Yeah!" Grace, Alex, and Candace cheered.

"Okay!" Priya said, raising her hands and taking a step back. "I was just—"

"Trying to help, we know," Gaby said sarcastically. "But you'd better not try it, Priya. I'm serious." She looked over at the rest of the Red team with fire in her eyes. "Any of you guys so much as trips on the obstacle course tomorrow and we're gonna know you threw it."

"And you'd better not. Because we're gonna beat you fair and square," Alex said firmly.

"Yeah!" the rest of the girls chorused. Tori smiled and sat up straight. This was kind of nice.

"We'll see about that!" Jenna said.

"Yeah, we won't hold back one bit!" Brynn added.

"Good!" Alex challenged.

"Good!" the girls on Red challenged back.

Tori laughed. Any second they were going to turn into kindergartners and start sticking their tongues out at one another. But instead, Priya sat down again and the entire Red team gathered into a huddle, whispering together. Probably going over strategy for the obstacle course.

"Wow, guys. Thanks," Tori said, turning to her team. "I had no idea you guys believed in me like that."

Alex frowned. "We haven't been that supportive, have we?"

"Well, I guess I could have been better, too," Tori said. "I should have listened to you guys on the dock that day. I was just trying to be a good leader, but I guess part of that is actually letting the team pitch in."

"We'll all be better from now on," Grace said, putting her hand over Tori's in the center of the table. "We're there for ya, captain."

"Yeah. We're there for ya," Candace said, putting her hand on top of Grace's.

"Totally," Alex said, adding her hand. "And we are going to win that obstacle course ribbon."

Everyone looked at Gaby. She rolled her eyes and sat forward. "This is cheesy, but okay. I'm here for you all, too," she said with a laugh.

Tori smiled and glanced over at Natalie. Hers was the only hand missing, and it kind of hurt that she wasn't there. But Tori didn't want to dwell on that now. For the first time in days, she was actually feeling good about her team.

*Let's see, what would a good captain do at this moment?* Tori thought. Then her grin widened.

"Blue team, on three. Ready?"

Her friends nodded.

"One, two three!"

"Blue team!" they all shouted, throwing their hands up.

All across the cafeteria, the other Blue team members cheered and hooted and hollered. Tori sat back in her chair feeling giddy. Maybe Belle was right. Maybe she *did* have strengths. And one of those strengths was her friends.

chapter

EIGHT

Tori stood at the obstacle course with the rest of her team while the fourth-division boys ran, crawled, rode, and climbed their way through the various challenges. Once again, she was faced with making a decision on which team member should take on which event, but this time she wasn't feeling so stressed about it. Now she knew she had the support of her teammates, and together they could take on anything.

"I think Alex should do the trike ride," Gaby said, as the entire crowd cheered a blond boy's successful scaling of the portable climbing wall. "She has the shortest legs."

"Hey!" Alex protested.

"What? You'll be able to work it better. My knees would hit the handlebars and tip me over," Gaby said with a shrug.

Tori glanced at Alex. Gaby's point did kind of make sense. "What do you think?"

"Fine. I'll do it," Alex said with a determined nod. "For the team."

Tori grinned. "I think Candace should do

the rock climbing, and Gaby—you've been killer at basketball this year. What do you guys think?"

"I'm in," Gaby said.

"I don't know. It's really high," Candace said, looking worriedly over Tori's shoulder.

"Well, it's either you, Grace, or Natalie," Tori said.

She looked over at Nat, who was standing somewhat to the side, staring into space. The moment Tori said her name, she started twirling her hair around her finger like she wasn't paying attention. Tori's heart constricted. She couldn't believe that in less than a week, she and Natalie had grown so far apart. Part of her wanted to ignore Natalie's existence, just like Natalie was doing to her, but she was the captain here. She was supposed to be the bigger person. Tori took a deep breath and swallowed her pride.

"Natalie, what do you want to do?" she asked.

"Whatever," Natalie said, not even bothering to look Tori in the eye. "I don't care."

Tori had to bite her tongue to keep from snapping at the girl. Why was she giving Tori attitude? Natalie was the one who had completely ditched Tori for someone else. Tori had a feeling that if Lainie were over here right now asking Natalie what she wanted to do in the obstacle course, Natalie would be volunteering for everything and being all super-positive. Anything to impress Queen Lainie.

"The one thing I don't want to do is the dizzy run," Grace put in. "I'll do anything else."

"Oh, yeah. Me too. Anything but the dizzy run,"

Candace echoed, sticking her tongue out.

Over near the course, the crowd whipped into a cheering frenzy, which meant the fourth-division boys were entering the last leg. Tori had to make her final decisions now.

"Okay, then Candace, you're on the wall. Grace, you do the egg run, and I'll . . ."

For a split second, Tori thought about doing the dizzy run herself—taking one for the team as the captain. But didn't she already do that with the pie-eating contest? When Natalie was basically nowhere to be found? She glanced again at Natalie, who was now casually inspecting her fingernails. Girl didn't want to participate in the team meeting? Then it was her loss.

"I'll do the tires and Nat can do the dizzy run," Tori said.

"What?" Natalie said, suddenly snapping to.

"You said you'd do 'whatever,'" Gaby pointed out before Tori even had a chance. She even threw in some air quotes for good measure.

Natalie narrowed her eyes, but said nothing.

"Fifth-division girls! Please take your places!" Dr. Steve called out through his megaphone.

"All right, Blue team!" Tori shouted, ignoring Natalie's stare of death. "Let's do this!"

"Yeah!" everyone cheered.

They all high-fived and clapped before walking off to take their places along the course. Tori stood in front of the tunnel o' tires and saw that she was up against Alyssa for the Red team. Alyssa, as uncompetitive as ever, raised her hand in a wave. Tori smiled and did the same. It was nice that some people were still normal around here. Of course, Tori was still planning on completely smoking Alyssa in her leg of the race. Thanks to the support of her friends, Tori had officially gotten the Color War bug.

"On your mark! Get set! Go!" Dr. Steve shouted.

Natalie stuck the bat to her forehead and spun around with Clarissa counting off her turns. When she dropped the bat, she took off to the right and everyone laughed. Luckily, on the other side, Chelsea had started running completely off the course.

"Go, Natalie! Go!" Alex screamed from the trike run. "Over here! Run to me!"

Natalie shook her head like she was trying to clear water out of her ears. That earned her another laugh from the crowd, but then she focused on Alex and took off in a staggering line. She was yards ahead of Chelsea, who had just figured out that she was *not* supposed to be approaching the steps of the nature shack.

"Go, Natalie!" Tori shouted, getting into the spirit. She may have been angry at Nat for personal reasons, but this was a team thing now.

Nat slapped Alex's hand, and Alex straddled the tricycle. She pedaled like a maniac, weaving in and out of the cones. Her face was set in a concentrated frown and she hunched low over the handlebars. She looked so funny, Tori couldn't help laughing through her cheers.

"Go, Alex! Rock that trike!" Tori shouted.

Alex got to the end of the winding course before Brynn ever even got onto her trike. She slapped Tori's hand, and Tori hit the deck. As she crawled through the snaking maze of tires, her knees scraped against silty rocks and rubber edges, but she took it all and kept going. When she stumbled out the far side, Alyssa was nowhere to be seen. Tori shoved herself to her feet and ran over to slap Candace's hand.

"Go! Go! Go!" she cried, catching her breath.

Candace turned, her brown hair flying, and started up the wall. It was slightly tilted to keep it from being too difficult, and Candace was doing well. But when she got halfway up the wall, she paused. Looking around in confusion, she clung to her spot.

"What's the matter?" Tori shouted up to her, glancing over at Alyssa, who had just slapped Valerie's hand.

"Where do I go?" Candace cried.

Tori studied the wall. Candace did have a problem. It looked like all the handholds were out of her reach. Valerie was catching up with her and the Red team fans were going nuts, cheering her on. Tori was just starting to see this competition, like all the others, going down the drain. But then her eye caught on a plan.

"Candace! Move to the right!" Tori shouted. "There's a clear path to the right!"

"Yeah?"

"Yeah! See the red foothold to your right? Go there!"

On the other rock wall, Valerie was climbing like

a pro. Candace held her breath and r̶
foot over. She grabbed a blue handhold
hand, then followed with her left leg and
she was secure, she looked up.

"See it? Grab the green handhold and
golden!" Tori cried. "Now go! Go! Go!"

"Okay!" Candace squealed.

And then she started to climb again. Like a
spider, she scurried up the wall so quickly it was as if
someone was chasing her. The second she reached the
top, Tori jumped up and down.

"Yeah, Candace! Good work!" Tori shouted.

Candace grinned. "Couldn't have done it without you!"

Tori welled with pride. Maybe she was good at
this captain thing after all.

Candace swung her legs over and slid down the
slide on the other side. She slapped Gaby's hand just
seconds before Valerie slapped Priya's.

"Go, Gaby! Go! You can do it!" Tori shouted.

Candace came over and clung to Tori's hand, and
soon Alex and Natalie were there as well. Tori glanced
at Nat's shouting face and thought that maybe, if they
could come together for this, everything could still
be okay. She wished things could just go back to the
way they were a week ago, before Color War had ever
started, when she and Natalie were still best friends.
Meanwhile, Gaby dribbled around the chairs set up on
the court, then threw her penalty shot at the end. It
swished right through the hoop.

"Yes! Yeah, Gaby! Yeah!" Tori shouted, raising

ndace's hand in the air.

Gaby smacked Grace's hand so hard, Grace
winced. But then she took her spoon and egg and took
off toward the finish line. Priya made her shot easily
and slapped Jenna's hand as well.

"Let's go!" Tori told her friends.

They all ran to the sidelines along the egg
run. Holding hands in a chain of five, they screamed
for Grace.

"Go, Grace!" they all shouted.

"Don't drop that egg!" Gaby added.

Grace bent at the knee, as if it would give her
more balance, and moved forward quickly. She looked
like a duck, but she was moving fast. Her lips were
pressed together as she concentrated on the egg. Jenna
meanwhile, jogged forward, a determined look in
her eye.

"Come on, Grace! Go!" Tori cried.

Then Jenna suddenly stopped and her eyes
widened. Everyone gasped as she got her balance.
She'd almost lost her egg! She righted herself and kept
running, but it was too late. Grace was a few feet from
the finish line.

"Go, Grace! Go Blue!" Tori cried, her heart
pounding in her ears.

Grace crossed the finish line and threw her
hands in the air as the entire Blue team went totally
insane. Her egg flew in a wide arc and landed with a
splat, right on top of Dr. Steve's one red shoe.

"Yes! We won!" Tori shouted. "We actually won!"
She ran toward Grace and threw her arms

around her friend. Her whole team gathe~~~~
hugging and cheering and hugging son~~~
glanced around for Natalie, but didn't see~~~
crowd. Maybe she'd been wrong about patchi~~~
up after all. Tori felt a pang of disappointment, bu~
decided she couldn't let Natalie get to her right now~

She had won her first Color War event! And sh~
was going to celebrate with the rest of her team.

▲ ▲ ▲

That afternoon before dinner, bunk 5A had
free time to write letters home. This time, Tori didn't
ask Natalie for some of her handmade stationery. She
simply took her plain old notebook and went outside
to the porch to write. Natalie's heart felt heavy as she
leaned back on her pillows. She lifted her pen to write
to her mother and tell her all about her new friend
and her potential boyfriend (Nat's mom was cool like
that), but she found she didn't much feel like gushing.
Instead, she pulled out the latest *Us Weekly*, which her
friends from home had sent her, and settled in to look
at the pictures.

"Uh, Natalie?"

Grace and Alex hovered over Natalie's bunk.

"Can we talk to you?" Alex asked.

"Sure," Nat said, laying the magazine aside.
"What's up?"

Together, Grace and Alex sat down near the
foot of Natalie's bunk, ducking under the upper cot.
They both had serious expressions on and Natalie felt a
thump of foreboding. Grace, for one, almost *never* looked

ous. Unless she was talking about school.

"Is this about Tori?" Natalie asked.

"Sort of," Alex said, pulling her knee up toward her chin and hugging her leg. "But really, it's about all of us. We've all sort of noticed you haven't been around much lately."

"Because you've been hanging out with Lainie," Grace put in.

"Yeah . . . ?" Natalie said.

Grace and Alex glanced at each other. "Well, we miss you for one," Alex said.

Natalie's heart squeezed a bit and she smiled. That was sweet.

"And we don't like Lainie, for another," Grace said.

"What?" Natalie blurted.

Okay. Forget sweet.

Alex whacked Grace's arm. "Ow!" Grace protested, holding the spot. "What did you *want* me to say?"

"You weren't supposed to put it like that!" Alex told her, rolling her dark eyes.

"You guys, why don't you like Lainie?" Natalie asked, feeling defensive. "So we're hanging out. So what? Big deal. I can have other friends, can't I?"

"Sure you can, Nat. It's just that we're not totally sure Lainie's really your friend," Alex said.

Natalie scoffed and leaned back on her pillows, crossing her arms over her chest. It was so clear what was going on here. They were just jealous of her. Jealous that she had a new, older, cooler friend.

"We're serious!" Grace said. "We've been here a lot longer than you, Natalie. We've known Lainie practically our entire lives."

"Yeah, and every year she does the same thing," Alex said, growing animated. "There's always someone who ends up getting dumped by her. Used and then dumped. She does it all the time. Every summer."

"You are so wrong," Natalie said, shaking her head. "Lainie's not like that."

"How do you know?" Alex asked. "I'm telling you. I've *seen* it happen. A bunch of times."

"I *know* because we're friends," Natalie told them firmly. "Real friends. She's not using me for anything. She tells me stuff. Stuff you wouldn't tell someone you were just planning on dumping."

"Okay, if you say so," Alex said doubtfully.

"I say so," Natalie told them. She swung her legs over the side of her bunk and headed for the bathroom. "But thanks for the warning," she said over her shoulder.

She saw the two of them exchange another look and she almost felt sorry for them. They were so clueless. Lainie was a cool girl. And no one was going to convince Natalie otherwise.

▲ ▲ ▲

"Are you nervous?" Natalie asked Lainie, watching her friend's foot tap-tap-tap against the floor.

Instantly, Lainie stopped tapping and stood up straight. "Nervous? Me? Why should I be nervous?"

"No reason," Natalie said with a smirk.

They were standing against the wall in the mess hall during the Color War Scrabble tournament. In the center of the room, six tables were set up with one Scrabble board on each. Four competitors played at each board—two guys and two girls from each division. Alex was representing the fifth-division Blue team along with Simon, Natalie's former boyfriend. At the same board were Alyssa and David from the Red team. They all looked very intense, but Natalie couldn't tell who was winning or losing. She had better things to concentrate on, anyway. Namely, helping Lainie land this Christopher guy.

"Are you sure the skirt looks okay?" Lainie asked, smoothing down the front of the blue cotton drawstring skirt she had borrowed from Trish.

"Yes. And it totally matches the NY on your shirt," Natalie said. "It's you, just dressier."

Lainie glanced down at the glittery interlocking NY on her white tank top. She was a big Yankees fan and when she had told Nat that this was her favorite shirt, Natalie had insisted that Lainie wear it for the big night. That way, she would be comfortable and confident. Then, right after dinner, they had met up outside the main hall so that Nat could brush out Lainie's long hair and add a little extra makeup to her eyes and cheeks. The result? Lainie looked like an utterly fabulous girly-tomboy. Boys *loved* utterly fabulous girly-tomboys. It was like the best of both worlds for them. A pretty girl they could hang out with at ballgames? Boy heaven.

"Okay, I'm gonna do it," Lainie said suddenly.

"I'm going over there and I'm going to talk to him."

"Good! You are *so* ready!" Natalie said.

Lainie lifted her eyebrows. "You think?"

"I know!" Natalie said with a giggle. "Just be yourself. Talk about Color War. Talk about sports. Ask him questions about him. Boys *love* to talk about themselves."

"Got it," Lainie said with a nod, already looking over Natalie's shoulder. "Thanks, Nat. I really owe you one."

Natalie's heart warmed. She wished Alex and Grace could have heard that. Those were not the words of a person who was *using* someone else.

"Good luck," Natalie said, giddily.

Lainie shook her long hair back over her shoulders and strode confidently across the room. Natalie watched her, feeling almost like a proud parent. No one ever would have known how nervous Lainie was. She as going to knock this Christopher kid right out of his flip-flops.

If he was wearing flip-flops, of course. Actually, Natalie couldn't wait to see what he was wearing, and what he looked like for that matter. Lainie's ultimate crush was about to be revealed.

"What's she up to?" Liliko asked, stepping up next to Natalie, along with Patty. They had been off flirting with their own set of cute boys, but had apparently noticed Lainie's cross-room journey.

"She's gonna talk to Christopher," Natalie whispered. "Which one is he?"

Just then, Lainie paused on the other side of the

room, right in front of a group of guys who were all chatting and laughing. She said a few words to one of them and he moved away from the wall to hear her better. At first, Natalie couldn't see him because Lainie was blocking him from sight. Natalie stood on her toes and craned her neck just as Lainie shifted her feet. Just like that, there he was. The boy of Lainie's dreams.

Logan.

Natalie's heart clenched. Lainie was talking to Logan. Blond, surferboy Logan. Natalie's potential BF, *Logan*.

"Wait a minute, that's not—" Natalie started.

"Omigod! Look at his face!" Patty exclaimed, grabbing Liliko's arm. "Chris is *totally* smitten."

Natalie's mouth snapped shut as she watched Lainie touch Logan's shoulder and tilt her head flirtatiously. Apparently Lainie's Christopher really *was* Logan. But how? How could this be happening? Natalie had no idea what was going on here, but whatever it was, it was not good.

chapter

# NINE

Natalie barely slept at all that night. She lay awake, staring at the bottom of Chelsea's bunk above her and toying with her platinum Tiffany ring. She just could not figure out how it was possible that *her* Logan was also *Lainie's* Christopher. Were there two of him? Twins? It just didn't make any sense. Lainie had said Christopher had green eyes, but Logan's were definitely blue. And she'd said he had light blond hair, but Logan's was more dark blond. Plus she'd said he was short, but Logan was definitely tall.

Of course, he might be short standing next to Lainie . . . she *was* a lot taller than Natalie. But still, that didn't explain the eyes and the hair. What was going on around here?

However it had happened, it seemed clear that Natalie and Lainie liked the same guy. Which made Natalie feel wretched and sour inside. She had to talk to Lainie. She had to make sure this wasn't all just some big mistake. If only they weren't in different divisions. If Lainie were a fifth-division camper, Natalie could just wake her up and whisper it all out right now. But instead, she was going to have to wait out the moon and the crickets before she could find an answer.

For the first time ever, Natalie was the first girl in her bunk up, showered, and ready to go in the morning. The second Belle said they could leave for breakfast, she was out the door and running. No one in her bunk was really talking to her, anyway. The Red team was being very cliquey, and the Blue team all seemed to resent her relationship with Lainie—a relationship she was pretty much desperate to save at this point.

Natalie raced along the throng of campers headed for the mess hall and caught sight of Lainie up ahead. The girl was hard to miss since she was so much taller than everyone else and had that thick braid of hair. Nat hooked a left and cut straight through the crowd.

"Ow! Watch it!" a sixth-division girl from the Red team cried as Natalie stepped on her sandaled foot.

"Sorry!" Natalie replied with a cringe.

She finally arrived, breathless and ruddy, at Lainie's side. Lainie, unfortunately, did not notice. She was too busy gushing to Liliko, Trish, Daniella, and Patty. Each one of them wore their blue T-shirts over gray or black Soffe shorts and colorful sneakers. It was as if the sixth-division had their very own uniforms.

"He was so *sweet*, you guys. You have no idea," Lainie was saying, placing both hands over her heart and looking up at the sky. "He even said I was doing a great job leading the Blue team. I couldn't believe he'd noticed!"

Natalie swallowed a huge lump of bitterness that had formed in her throat. "Hey, guys," she croaked.

Lainie turned around and her eyes brightened. "Natalie! Hey! There you are! I was just telling the girls how great Christopher was last night."

"Apparently he *loved* the outfit you picked out," Trish told Natalie.

"Who knew Chris was so into jocks?" Daniella said, then snickered.

"He said he likes a girl who shows her team spirit," Lainie confirmed.

"Yeah? That's just . . . fab," Natalie said awkwardly. "So, Christopher . . . he was the guy with the blond hair? The one that always wears that necklace with the medallion?"

*Please let her say no. Please let her say she was just talking to Logan* before *she found Christopher.*

"Yep! That's him! Isn't he *such* the hottie?" Lainie gushed, her face shining with happiness.

Natalie felt hot tears of confusion and jealousy sting her eyes and she looked straight ahead. "Yeah. He sure is," she managed to say. "I thought you said he had *light* blond hair, though. Isn't his more dark?"

"You think? I think it's pretty light," Lainie replied. "Anyway, who cares? The point is, we're going to sit together at the singdown on the last night of Color War. It's gonna be so romantic. The dark, the fire, him and me all cuddled in together . . ."

"Sigh," Liliko said dreamily.

"Sounds perfect," Patty put in. "You should have done this ages ago, Lainie. You two are going to be the

Camp Lakeview power couple."

Lainie giggled and preened. "You know it!"

Natalie's heart squeezed painfully at the thought of Lainie and Christopher/Logan being *any* kind of couple, power or no. And she couldn't help noticing that Lainie had yet to thank her for her help. Not that she hadn't thanked her the night before, but Natalie would have thought that she would have said something now—considering how happy she was.

"Well, better go," Lainie said as they walked into the mess hall together. "See ya later, Nat!"

"Yeah!" Natalie said, watching as the sixth-division girls hustled off together, laughing and chatting. Then the fifth-division girls came in behind her, doing the same. Suddenly she felt very alone.

"See ya," she muttered.

▲ ▲ ▲

Priya sat at a table in the newspaper cabin, updating the scores and stats from all the Color War events that had taken place so far so that the list could be printed in the next issue. She was very aware of the fact that Tori was in the room, and even more aware of the fact that Tori hadn't spoken a word to her since the day before. Just then, Tori was on the other side of the cabin chatting with Dana. Priya wished she could just go over there and apologize to Tori again, but she had a feeling it would get her nowhere. Or that Tori would yell at her right in front of everyone. That didn't sound like fun.

"Priya!" Dana called suddenly. She got up from

her chair and hustled over to Priya's table, with Tori following reluctantly behind. Dana had a pencil behind each ear, making her hair stick out messily, and her blue T-shirt was wrinkled beyond belief. She was not a girl who cared much about appearances. "You didn't tell me that you and Tori were both captains of your Color War teams!"

Priya glanced at Tori, who set her jaw and looked quickly away. Where was this going?

"Yeah. We are," Priya said. "Should I have told you that?"

"Of course you should have!" Dana exclaimed. "This is the perfect opportunity for a special column. The experiences of two captains from the same cabin. Opposing views, one Red, one Blue. It'll be like a she said, she said. You know?"

Priya stared at Dana, baffled. No, she didn't know. In fact, she had no idea what Dana was talking about. But she knew from experience that the more Dana tried to explain an idea, the more confusing the idea usually became. "Uh . . . sure. I guess," she said.

"Great! Now get to it, you two!" Dana slapped both Tori and Priya on their backs, then walked over to her computer.

Tori and Priya locked eyes. Priya felt all uncertain and shaky inside. What was she supposed to do here? Try to apologize again? The last time she had done that she'd gotten her head bitten off. Then Tori blew out a sigh and sat down.

"Sorry. I was just talking to her and now we're doomed," Tori said, pulling her blond hair forward over her shoulder and slumping.

Priya's heart warmed. Tori was talking to her again!

"I don't care about the stupid assignment. We'll deal with it," Priya said. "I just don't want you to be mad at me anymore. I'm so sorry if I hurt your feelings."

Tori took a deep breath and wrapped some hair tightly around her finger, staring at her fingertip as it turned bright red. "I just never thought you were like that," she said quietly.

"Like what?" Priya asked.

"All egotistical," Tori said matter-of-factly, dropping the hair. "Like you're the best or whatever."

Priya felt as if she'd just been slapped. "Whoa. Was that how I was acting?"

"Kind of," Tori said, looking at her for the first time. "You thought your team was so great that the only way I could win was if you *let* me win. I mean, come on."

Priya swallowed hard. She placed her pencil down on the table and stared at it. She hadn't thought of it that way. She had just thought she was helping Tori out. But Tori was right. It took a pretty inflated head to think that *trying* to lose was the only way to help Tori.

"Man. I guess I really let the captain thing get to my head, huh?" Priya said.

"Kind of," Tori said with a small smile.

"I am *so* sorry, Tori," Priya said. "You must hate me for ever suggesting we throw an event."

"I don't hate you," Tori said. "I know that your

heart was in the right place. You only wanted to make me feel better. But just so we're clear, from here on out, I don't need any help. The Blue team is going to be fine."

Priya smiled, impressed. "Good attitude."

"Thought you'd like that," Tori said, grinning now.

That one smile told Priya all she needed to know. Whatever happened in the Color War, everything was going to be fine between her and Tori. She felt as if someone had just lifted a wet towel off her shoulders.

"So, any idea what we're supposed to do with this column?" Tori asked finally, picking up a pen and pad.

"Not a clue," Priya said, turning in her seat to face the desk. "But I'm sure that as long as we work on it together, it'll be awesome."

"Can someone pass the sandwiches?" Jenna shouted down the table at lunch.

"I don't think so," Gaby replied, pulling the platter closer to herself. "You eat any more grilled cheese and you're gonna turn into one."

Tori laughed along with her other Blue team members. They were all giddy today, psyched for the next Color War event. They had no idea what it would be, but for the first time Tori really felt like they could win it—whatever it was. And she knew her friends were feeling that way, too.

"Hey! You can't hoard the food!" Jenna said,

kneeling on her chair. "Belle! The Blue team's trying to hoard the food!"

"No hoarding the food, girls," Belle said, not looking up from her clipboard.

"Tattletale," Gaby said under her breath. She shoved the platter toward the other end of the table.

"Yeah! Tattletale!" Candace echoed.

"Sticks and stones may break my bones, but I got the cheese!" Jenna sang. She grabbed a half of a sandwich and ripped into it with a smile. The rest of the Red team laughed.

"Does she *ever* stop eating?" Gaby asked under her breath.

"Sure she does. Once she eats right through all the food *and* the plate and her teeth hit the table," Grace joked. "Then she *definitely* stops."

Alex reached over to high-five Grace.

"Hey! They're talking about me!" Jenna said, pointing at them. "Belle, make them stop talking about me!"

"You're on your own there, kid," Belle replied.

"Now, ladies, we don't need to talk about the Red team," Tori said, folding her hands primly on the table. "They already know how superior we are to them."

"Oh!" the Red team shouted.

"That is so *wrong!*" Brynn cried.

"Aw, yeah!" Alex said.

"Woot! Woot!" Grace said, pumping her hands in the air.

Gaby smacked hands with Tori, and Candace did the same. Tori glanced at Natalie, who glanced quickly away. Why did she refuse to get involved in the fun? Tori just could not figure it out. Was it because the sixth-division girls were too cool to high-five and woot-woot? Tori could hardly believe that less than a week ago *she* was the one that thought all this stuff was immature and *Natalie* was telling her to get in the spirit.

"Can I have everyone's attention, please?" Dr. Steve called out suddenly, his megaphone letting out a shriek. Everyone winced and groaned, but quickly quieted. These days, when Dr. Steve spoke, it was all about Color War. The entire camp turned its attention to the head table at the front of the room. Dr. Steve stood behind his chair with his megaphone.

"It's time for a Color War update," Dr. Steve said, looking down at a card in his hand. "As of right now, the standings are as follows. Blue team, you have 210 points."

The Blue team erupted in applause throughout the room. Tori clapped as hard as anyone.

"Red team, you have 300 points!"

The roar of the Red team was deafening. Tori narrowed her eyes as the girls at the other end of the table went absolutely nuts, dancing and bumping hips with each other. So unsophisticated. She could understand if Natalie didn't want to participate in displays like *that*.

"But there is still *plenty* of time for the Blue team to catch up!" Dr. Steve announced to a chorus of cheers and jeers. "Now tomorrow, we're going to do something a little different. Our next Color War event will be an arts and crafts event!"

"An arts and crafts event?" Alex said, her brow creasing. "What's that?"

Tori was confused. If Alex didn't know what something at camp was, then it didn't exist.

"For the first time, you're going to get to put all the skills you've learned in arts and crafts to good use in Color War," Dr. Steve continued. "Each team will have to conceptualize and construct a project that reflects the spirit of Camp Lakeview. And you'll have all night to work on it. Tomorrow afternoon, we'll have a presentation right here in the mess hall. You'll be judged on creativity and how well we think you've represented the camp. So have fun, and good luck!"

Dr. Steve switched off his megaphone and Tori turned to her team. Unfortunately, they were all busy slumping in their chairs.

"Well, we're dead," Grace said, blowing a curl of red hair out of her face.

"What? Why?" Tori asked.

"They have Alyssa," Gaby said, throwing her hand up toward the Red team and letting it slap back down. Sure enough, the Red team was already gathered in a huddle around Alyssa herself. "She's the most artistic girl in camp."

"Hey. A lot of us are artistic," Tori said. "We just have to come up with an original idea. Something spectacular. Something no one would expect."

"Yeah, that'll be easy," Gaby said.

"It's gonna be hard," Candace agreed.

"Not if we put our heads together," Tori said,

glancing at Natalie, who was staring off into space. "Now, what represents the spirit of Camp Lakeview?"

"Bug juice?" Alex suggested, lifting her cup of red punch.

Everyone laughed. Over Alex's shoulder, Tori caught a glimpse of Nurse Carrie getting up to go talk to Dr. Steve, those scrubs of hers as baggy and blah as ever. That woman could really use a new wardrobe.

Wait a minute . . . that was it! Suddenly Tori was hit with an amazing idea. Could it work? Belle had told her to play to her strengths. She had a feeling that with a little creativity and hard work, she just might be able to pull it off.

"Ladies," she said, leaning in toward the table. "I think I've got it."

chapter

# TEN

"Hey, Nat. Are you okay?"

Natalie glanced over her shoulder to find Alex jogging to catch up with her. They were walking to the lake for ghost story night, and Natalie had thought everyone in her cabin was ahead of her, their flashlights bobbing along the trees. Lately it had been her habit to drop back to the rear of the pack so that she could look for Lainie. Tonight, however, she'd done it so that she could look for Logan/Christopher and maybe get some answers. Still, somehow Alex had ended up behind her.

"Yeah. I'm fine," Natalie said distractedly. She looked past Alex's baseball cap into the dark, trying to make out the faces of the guys to their left. They looked too young and scrawny to be sixth-division boys, though. "Why? Do I look not-okay?"

"Actually, you seem kind of . . . out of it lately. Especially tonight. If you don't mind me saying," Alex told her.

Natalie looked into Alex's concerned eyes

and almost laughed. Leave it to Alex to always get right to the point.

"If it's about what Grace and I said about Lainie, I'm really sorry," Alex said. "If you say you guys are real friends, then I'm sure you are."

"Thanks," Natalie said, her heart warming slightly. Alex was the first and only person to try to understand Natalie's new friendship, and she appreciated it. Maybe she should talk to Alex about what was going on. It could be good to get it off her chest and hear someone else's opinion. Unfortunately, just as she was about to spill her guts, Nat finally spotted Logan/Christopher on the other side of the pathway. Her heart caught in her throat. She couldn't risk losing him in the crowd now. "But I gotta go," she said quickly. "I'll see you later."

She had just enough time to see Alex's face fall before she took off. Darn it. Now she was going to have someone else mad at her. But she would have to deal with that later. She *had* to find out what was up with the double-named boy.

Natalie grabbed Logan/Christopher's arm and yanked him right off the pathway into the woods. A couple of the other sixth-division boys shouted in surprise, but no one tried to stop her.

"Hey!" Logan/Christopher said with a laugh. "This is so totally against the rules."

Still, he followed her a few steps into the trees. Natalie caught her breath and glanced over her shoulder to see if anyone had noticed their escape other than his pals. A few yards away, dozens of pairs of sneakers tromped by and laughter wafted up toward the sky, mixed with various Color War chants. They were safe.

"Wow. You must have really missed me, Lee," Logan/Christopher said, lowering his voice in a way that made Natalie feel warm all over. Suddenly she was very aware that she was alone in the dark with her crush, and he was standing so close to her that she could see the weave in his polo shirt. But she had to ignore that. This was *not* supposed to be a romantic moment. Nat had questions and she wanted answers.

"Hang on there a second," Natalie said. She placed her hand on his shoulder and pushed him back until her elbow was locked. "There's something I need to know." A little line formed between his eyebrows and, if possible, he looked cuter than ever. Suddenly she realized that there was no telling whether his eyes were blue or green. What was up with that? "What color are your eyes?"

Somehow, he looked even more baffled. "They're sort of blue-green. They change depending on what I'm wearing. Why?"

Oh, God. Things were starting to fall into place. "Okay, is your name Logan, or is it Christopher?"

"It's both," he said. "It's Christopher Logan."

"What?" Natalie blurted. "I thought your *first* name was Logan."

"That's just what the guys call me. We all use our last names," he said, only growing more confused. "What's the problem?"

Natalie felt as if her mind was whirling. So it was definitely true. She liked the same boy Lainie had liked for the last six years. Which only meant one thing.

"The problem is . . . I like you," Natalie said reluctantly.

Christopher smiled. "How is that a problem?"

"It's a problem because I can't talk to you anymore," Natalie said, drooping back against a thick tree trunk.

Christopher pushed his hands into the pockets of his shorts. "Okay, now I'm confused."

"Look, Lainie likes you, too. And I just couldn't do that to her," Natalie said, feeling awful even as she said it. "She's my friend."

"Lainie Wilcox? But I don't like Lainie Wilcox," Christopher said, making a dubious face. "She's like one of the guys."

"What?" Natalie said, feeling suddenly defensive on her friend's behalf. "She is *so* not a guy! She's totally beautiful."

Christopher took a step closer to Natalie and her heart pounded like crazy. "I happen to think someone else is totally beautiful," he said.

Natalie's breath caught in her throat. He couldn't be talking about her, could he? But before she could even start breathing again, Christopher reached for her hand.

"Oh! My! *God!*"

Christopher sprung backward and Natalie's heart hit her throat. Two flashlight beams were pointed right at her from the break in the trees she and Christopher had ducked into. The flashlights were held by none other than Patty and Daniella. Slowly,

Daniella's face twisted into an evil smirk.

"You are *so* dead."

Natalie's stomach clenched painfully. "You guys—"

But it was too late. Patty and Daniella had already run off.

▲ ▲ ▲

"I just think it'll be so much more visually cool than a painting," Alyssa said as the Red team huddled around her sketches at the campfire. "But what do you guys think?"

"I love it," Priya said, leaning forward. Her butt was cold from sitting on the cool sand, so she balanced on the knees of her sweatpants for a little while. "I wish I could come up with ideas like you do, Lyss."

"It's not that big a deal," Alyssa said with a shrug. "We all have a million ideas inside us. At least that's what my art teacher is always saying."

"Well, it's totally going to slay whatever the Blue team comes up with," Jenna said confidently.

"Speaking of," Chelsea said, glancing up. She grabbed Alyssa's sketchbook right out of her hands and slapped it closed. Priya was about to scold her when she saw that the entire Blue team, minus Natalie, was walking by. They were keeping their steps very close to Priya's circle, too.

"How are you guys?" Tori asked, standing on her toes and looking into the circle. "Working on something there?"

"Maybe," Priya said. She leaned back on her

hands, all casual. "What about you? Working on something?"

"Maybe," Tori shot back. "Or maybe we're already done."

"Yeah right," Brynn said with a scoff.

Tori and the other girls looked at one another and grinned. Priya felt her heart skip a beat and she sat up straight again.

"You're *not* done, are you?" she asked.

Team Blue was silent for just a second, then they all cracked up laughing. Instantly, Priya relaxed.

"No, but you should have seen the look on your face!" Gaby said through her laughter.

"Ha ha ha," Jenna said, slinging her arm over Alyssa's shoulder. "Well if you guys think you can beat our secret weapon, you've got another think coming."

"We'll see," Tori said lightly.

Then she and the rest of the Blue team turned and walked over to another log, where they gathered together in a huddle. Planning their own arts and crafts project, no doubt.

"Yeah! We *will* see!" Jenna shouted after them.

Alyssa took her sketchbook back from Chelsea and opened it again. She pulled a metal tin of colored pencils out of the big pocket on the front of her sweatshirt and started to draw. "What if we do this . . . ?"

Priya was about to return her attention to the sketchbook when she finally spotted Natalie. She was sitting on a rock by herself, staring over at the sixth-division girls on the other side of the fire. Priya followed Natalie's gaze, wondering what Nat found so fascinating about the older girls. They didn't seem all that special to Priya. They all dressed alike, for one—no originality whatsoever. Plus they walked around with their noses in the air all the time, like they ran the place. When she and her friends got to the sixth division, they were *not* going to act like that. She knew that for sure.

Suddenly there was a commotion on the other side of the fire and Priya saw Natalie flinch. A bunch of campers in the area fell silent as Lainie Wilcox got up, shouting something about backstabbing. Then her counselor came over to calm her down and the two of them walked off together, Lainie still ranting.

"What was *that* all about?" Chelsea asked.

"Drama queens," Brynn said, rolling her eyes. That made everyone laugh, since Brynn was the biggest drama queen they knew.

Priya glanced back at Natalie. The girl's face was now as white as a marshmallow. Something told her that Nat knew exactly what that was all about.

▲ ▲ ▲

Natalie waited on the front porch of bunk 5A the next morning while everyone else showered and got ready. Her pulse was racing so fast she could barely sit still, so instead she paced back and forth, the wooden boards creaking beneath her feet. She knew what she had to do, she just wished she wasn't so nervous about it. The moment she saw Lainie and her friends walk by in the distance, she took a deep breath and told herself to just get it over with. She jogged down the steps and approached.

Lainie was flanked on one side by Liliko and Patty, and on the other side by Daniella and Trish. None of them even glanced at her when she arrived, even though Natalie could tell they knew she was there. She decided to ignore the other girls and get straight to the point, Alex style.

"Lainie, can I talk to you?"

Lainie said nothing. She didn't even blink. Just kept walking straight ahead. Nat's nervousness kicked it up a notch. She was glad she hadn't eaten anything yet, because she was starting to feel ill.

"Fine, you don't have to talk to me. Just listen," Natalie said, practically jogging to keep up with their long strides. "I didn't know his name was Christopher. All his friends call him Logan. But the second I found out he was the same guy, I told him I couldn't talk to him anymore."

Daniella let out a short laugh and Trish shot her a silencing look. Natalie rolled her eyes. She ran ahead and walked backward in front of Lainie. There was no way she could ignore Natalie when they were face-to-face.

"You have to believe me! We were just talking and I was telling him I couldn't be around him anymore!"

"You're such a little liar," Patty said. "We saw him holding your hand."

"Well, maybe he reached for my hand, but he wasn't *holding* it!" Natalie protested.

Lainie upped her pace and stepped right around Natalie. Nat stopped in her tracks. She couldn't believe this. Lainie wasn't even trying to understand. She wasn't even listening to her. What kind of person *was* she?

"I thought we were friends!" Natalie shouted, earning curious glances from a bunch of other campers on their way to the mess hall.

Lainie stopped and turned around. Natalie saw her chance.

"What happened to all that stuff about thinking alike and sharing the same brain and you wanting me to be in sixth division?" Natalie asked.

It took two steps for Lainie to get right in Natalie's face. "Well, you're not in sixth division, are you? And next time maybe I'll think twice about trusting a fifth-division loser," she said vehemently.

Natalie felt as if Lainie had just smacked her across the face. "Lainie—"

"No. Just listen," Lainie said. "Christopher Logan is going to be *mine*. Thanks to you, I finally got his attention," she added smugly. "And he *will* be my boyfriend by the end of the summer."

So Lainie *had* been using her. Just like Alex and Grace had warned her she would. The camp whirled around Natalie, a mess of colors and sounds and smells. She felt off balance, confused, and really, *really* stupid. It was like she was doing the obstacle course dizzy run all over again.

*There's always someone who ends up getting dumped by her. Used and then dumped,* Alex had said. *She does it all the time. Every summer.*

"And if I see you anywhere near him again, you're dead," Lainie added.

"I can't believe this," Natalie said, finding her

voice. "I can't believe you're really like this."

"Well, believe it," Lainie said, crossing her arms over her chest. She looked proud of herself, which just made Nat feel even more ill. "Now why don't you go back to your little fifth-division buddies where you belong and leave . . . me . . . alone," Lainie said through her teeth.

The other four girls behind her laughed and Lainie straightened up with a thin, mean smile. Then she turned and rejoined her friends, who all whispered together and then cracked up laughing again as they walked toward the mess hall.

# chapter ELEVEN

Natalie sat on the edge of her bunk, her hands pressed into her sheets as she watched the rest of the Blue team whispering and gathering materials together from their cubbies and suitcases. The entire camp had been given a free period that morning to work on their Color War projects, and the Red team had taken off to work in the arts and crafts cabin, letting the Blue team have the bunk. With everything that had been going on, Natalie had only just realized that she had no idea what her team was doing for the arts and crafts competition. No one had bothered to tell her, but she also hadn't bothered to ask. Her heart felt heavy as she watched them all laughing and conspiring as if she wasn't even there. She felt totally invisible. Plus she was still upset over her argument with Lainie. How was it possible that so many people hated her all at once?

"Okay, I'll run over to Adam's cabin and see if they have anything we can use," Alex said. "I'll be right back."

"We'll be working on the porch," Tori told her.

"Cool." Alex jogged out the door and Tori, Gaby, Candace, and Grace all turned to follow, their arms full of clothes and shoes.

Natalie screwed up her courage and stood. "What're you guys doing?"

There was just the slightest bit of hesitation in their steps, but then Tori shoved through the screen door. Candace and Grace, at least, managed to shoot Natalie apologetic glances before they went after her.

"Heard you had a big fight with Queen Lainie," Gaby said. "Is that why you're suddenly talking to us again?"

Then she turned and pushed the door open, letting it slam behind her before Natalie could even answer.

Natalie dropped back onto her bed and lay down. As much as she hated to admit it, Gaby had a point. Nat hadn't made much of an effort to be a teammate *or* a friend this past week. She knew that if Lainie hadn't shot her down, she'd probably still be trying to find a way to go over there and hang out with sixth division. She'd really messed things up. The question was, how could she fix them?

The door creaked open and Candace slid into the cabin. Natalie sat up as Candace came right over and sat down at her feet. Natalie looked at her, surprised, and waited to see what was going to happen next.

"They're pretty mad," Candace whispered finally.

"I know. I can tell," Natalie replied.

"I mean, I get it," Candace said, picking at a piece of lint stuck to Nat's sheet. "Everyone wants to hang out with the sixth-division girls, but you didn't have to dump everyone else in the meantime."

Natalie blinked, shocked. This was so *not* Candace.

"Why are you telling me this?" she asked.

"Because I hate when people are mad at one another," Candace said, squirming slightly. "It makes me feel all gross."

"So what do you think I can do?" Natalie whispered, scooting forward. "No one will talk to me."

"I don't know. I think you have to try to find a way to show Tori and them that you still care about the team. And about them," Candace said. "If they won't listen, then *do* something."

"Like what?" Natalie asked.

"Well, maybe you can get involved with the project?" Candace suggested.

"But I just asked what you guys were doing and Tori wouldn't even answer me," Natalie replied, feeling pathetic.

"We're doing a fashion show," Candace told her.

"A fashion show?" Natalie repeated. What a cool idea! And something she would totally love to help with. If only they'd let her. "What can I do to help?"

"I don't know. Maybe ask Tori?" Candace said.

Natalie clucked her tongue. "But she won't talk to me. You saw her."

"Then maybe *show* her how much you want to help," Candace said, getting up. "I don't know. I can't think of everything. But I hope you can come up with something, because this whole thing is making me way too tense."

She turned and started for the bathroom. Natalie's brain was already working, trying to figure out what she could do to make Tori and the others see how sorry she was. How could she use this new information? Information she wouldn't even have if it weren't for the person who was usually the quietest and *least* informative of the bunch.

"Candace?" she said.

Candace paused at the door to the bathroom and looked back.

"Thanks. You're a good friend," Natalie said.

Candace grinned from ear to ear. "No problem."

"What are we going to do?" Grace said, slumping back against the outer wall of bunk 5A. "We've got it all down except this one."

"Maybe we should just cut it out," Alex suggested. "I think we have enough outfits without it."

"No! We can't cut it out," Tori protested, digging through the spare clothing they had left in their pile. "It's what inspired me to do this in the first place. There has to be *something* we can use."

Suddenly the screen door was kicked open and everyone jumped. Tori's hand flew to her heart in surprise as Natalie stepped out of the cabin. At least, she thought it was Natalie. All she could see was a pair of skinny legs sticking out beneath a huge mound of clothing.

"Uh, is that Nat or the infamous fashion monster of Fifth Avenue?" Grace joked.

Tori gave her a sour look and Grace glanced down at the porch. Had Grace forgotten that Natalie was a traitor around here?

"No. It's me," Natalie said. She stepped forward, peeking around her pile of clothing so that she wouldn't crush anyone's hands beneath her feet, then dropped the whole mess in the center of the circle. A sweater fell over Gaby's head and Nat whipped it off, throwing it back on the mound. "I want you guys to have all this."

Tori's eyes widened and instantly she was thinking about all the cool stuff they could do with Natalie's vast wardrobe at their disposal. But she quickly pushed the thought aside.

"What makes you think we need your clothes?" she said.

"I know you're doing a fashion show," Natalie said, glancing at Candace, whose face got all blotchy. "I . . . overheard you talking."

"Yeah?" Tori said.

"Well, I don't know how you're making it represent Camp Lakeview or whatever, but if my clothes will help, you can have all of them," Natalie said.

"You're kidding," Alex said, her eyes wide. "Your clothes are your favorite thing."

"I know, but for you guys, I'll give them up," Natalie said. She looked Tori in the eye. "I know I've been a jerk for the past few days, but now I've remembered who my *real* friends are. You guys. All of you. And for that I will sacrifice my wardrobe," she said, holding her hands out.

Tori felt a little tickle in her heart as Natalie stared at her. She knew how important Natalie's clothes were to her. It had to take a lot for her to make a gesture like this.

"Wow," Grace said with a whistle. "That's major."

Everyone laughed. Even Tori and Natalie. But still, Tori couldn't entirely wipe the last week from her mind. All the times Natalie should have been there and wasn't. All week, Tori had felt hurt and let down by the person who was supposed to be her best friend. It wasn't that easy to forget.

"Now will you please, *please* let me help?" Natalie asked, clasping her hands together. "I told you I would be there for you, Tori, and I wasn't. Please let me make it up to you now."

Everyone looked at Tori. She could tell that they were all hoping she would put an end to this already. It was up to her to smooth it over and make sure they were all friends again. She looked at Natalie, who raised her eyebrows pleadingly, looking like a lost puppy dog. For some reason, that thought made Tori smile.

"Okay, fine," she said finally. "You can help."

The whole Blue team cheered.

"Yay! Thank you! Thank you *so* much! I swear I'll never do anything like this again," Natalie said.

"Yeah, yeah. Let's get back to work already," Gaby said. "Sit your butt down."

Natalie laughed, and Grace and Candace moved

apart so that Natalie could join the circle. Then Tori leaned over the pile of fresh clothes and glanced around to make sure there were no Red team spies lingering near the porch. The coast was clear.

"Now, let me tell you what we're planning to do . . ."

chapter

# TWELVE

"Wow. You guys did a really incredible job," Priya's friend Spence said, admiring the diorama Priya's team had constructed for the arts and crafts event. It was a miniature replica of the camp in 3-D, but thanks to Alyssa's huge paint set, the lake was psychedelic pink, the trees were purple, the grass was aqua, the sand was green, and the cabins were yellow. All to represent the originality of the camp. "It's so cool. Who came up with these colors?"

"That would be Alyssa," Priya said, as Alyssa gave a playful bow.

"Well, you've made the Red team proud, Alyssa," Spence said with a grin. "All we've got over there is a Camp Lakeview sign made out of Popsicle sticks."

The girls all stood on their toes to catch a glimpse of Spence's team's project a few tables down. All the different divisions and teams had been given a table in the mess hall on which to display their work. The judges circulated the room, jotting down scores on their clipboards as they went along, and most of the campers were checking out other people's projects. The various teams had created everything from posters to sculptures to mobiles and maps. Compared to all the other projects, Spence's team's work did look rather childish, and not at all stable. Sometimes the guys in the fifth division didn't seem to take anything seriously, unless it was sports.

"It's . . . original," Priya said, trying to be nice. After all, she'd had a crush on Spence all summer. She couldn't tell him to his adorable face that there was no way his project was going to win.

"And it definitely captures the spirit of camp," Gaby put in. "They're always getting us to make stuff out of Popsicle sticks. We even used some in our project." She pointed out the cabins, which were made out of painted Popsicle sticks.

Spence laughed. "Thanks for trying, you guys, but we all know it stinks."

He glanced over his shoulder as Dr. Steve approached with two counselors. "Uh-oh. Judges coming. Better go. Good luck, you guys! Not that you'll need it," he said, glancing at the empty table next to Priya's. "Where *is* the Blue team, anyway?"

"No one knows," Brynn said. "Maybe they bailed because they knew how very awesome our project was going to be."

"Yeah. They couldn't deal with us rubbing it in their faces," Jenna said with a crazy, devilish laugh.

Spence's eyes went wide. "Wow. I'm glad I'm on *your* side," he said before walking off.

"Jenna, maybe you should tone it down a little,"

Alyssa said under her breath. "You're starting to scare people."

"Starting?" Chelsea put in with an eye roll.

"Fifth-division girls Red team!" Dr. Steve announced as his troupe of judges stepped up to their table. He held up his clipboard so that they couldn't see what he'd written down so far. "What have you got for us?"

"It's a diorama of Camp Lakeview," Priya said proudly.

"My! How lovely!" Helene exclaimed, leaning toward the delicate structure. Helene was the ceramics instructor at Camp Lakeview and everyone knew she appreciated a wild color scheme. All she ever wore were batik-print shirts and flowing pants in crazy arrays.

Jeremy, the woodworking instructor, pushed his glasses higher up on his nose. "Interesting construction," he said. "What materials did you use?"

"Mostly construction paper, paint, and balsa wood," Alyssa piped in. "But there were some Popsicle sticks involved as well," she added with a smile.

"Balsa? Very delicate. This must have been difficult to put together," Jeremy said with a smile. "Well done, ladies."

He made a few notes on his clipboard and Jenna craned her neck, trying to see.

"Yes. Very well done. Very well done," Dr. Steve said, making a few marks himself. "Extra points for originality, girls."

Priya beamed and grabbed Alyssa's hand for a squeeze.

"Now on to fifth-division girls Blue team," Dr. Steve announced, turning to the next table. He stopped short when he saw that it was totally empty except for the blue handwritten sign that said FIFTH DIVISION GIRLS. "Where's the rest of your division, girls?" he asked Priya and the others.

Priya's mouth opened, but no sound came out. She had no clue where her friends had gone off to. But at that moment, the door to the mess hall was flung open and Tori ran in. Her face was red and beads of sweat dotted her hairline. She raced to her table and stood there, out of breath. Instantly Priya's heart went out to Tori. Clearly, she had nothing. Her hands were empty and she was gasping for breath in a panic. The last thing Priya wanted was for Tori and her team to be humiliated all over again.

"Blue team? Where is your project?" Dr. Steve asked. Helene eyed Tori as if the girl might spontaneously combust.

Tori took a deep breath. "If you'll follow me, Dr. Steve. Our presentation was a little big for the room, so we've set it up just outside."

A hush fell across the room, and Priya gave Jenna an ominous shrug.

"This should be interesting," Chelsea said under her breath.

"This had better not be some kind of prank, young lady," Dr. Steve said, narrowing his eyes. "Your division does have a reputation for that type of thing," he added, glancing at Jenna.

"It's not. I promise," Tori assured him. "I just really

need you to come outside."

Dr. Steve picked up his megaphone, which dangled from a strap over his shoulder, and flipped it on. "All right then, everyone! Fifth-division girls Blue team has a special presentation for us outside. So let's all head out in an orderly fashion, please!"

Priya, surprised and excited, was the first one out the door.

▲ ▲ ▲

Natalie, Tori, Gaby, Alex, and Candace all huddled together behind one of the bigger oaks—their "staging area"—as Grace strutted down their makeshift runway, which was really just two lines drawn in the dirt outside the mess hall. The whole camp had gathered along the sides of the runway, and they cheered as Grace—dressed in a Harvard sweatshirt, Candace's reading glasses, and a pair of pencils above her ears—struck a pose, then turned around and started walking back. With hair just as wild as Dana the newspaper counselor's, the two could have been twins.

Next was Alex, who went out there dressed up as Jeremy, in one of Adam's plaid shirts and a pair of thick sunglasses with the lenses popped out. Then Gaby mimicked Pete the cook's loping walk perfectly in a tie-dyed T-shirt and baggy jeans. And Candace totally pulled off Helene, wearing a batik T-shirt she had made in arts and crafts the year before. The camp was loving every minute of it.

"Okay, Nat! You're up!" Tori said.

"Here goes nothing," Natalie said.

She high-fived Candace as her friend returned to the staging area, and stepped out onto the runway. She wore a pair of old hospital scrubs she'd been using as pajama bottoms ever since they became trendy back in fifth grade. Her mother had gotten them from a doctor friend of hers and given them to Natalie as part of her birthday gift that year, and even though they were no longer trendy, Nat couldn't give them up. They were just too comfortable. Over them she wore a huge V-neck T-shirt of Gaby's that was roughly the same color, and her hair was back in a messy bun. Around her neck she wore a stethoscope made out of—what else—Popsicle sticks and a spool of thread.

Everyone applauded and Nurse Carrie blushed as Natalie walked by. Nat was grinning like crazy as she struck a pose at the far end of the runway. This was really working. Tori's idea had turned out incredibly well. She was just about to turn around and strut back to her friends when her eyes fell on Christopher in the crowd. Christopher talking to Lainie, to be exact. Natalie's heart dropped into her white Keds.

Lainie laughed and touched Christopher's chest, and he laughed as well. For a long, long moment, Natalie couldn't move. He didn't like Lainie, huh? Didn't think she was pretty, did he? Well it didn't look like that to her.

"Natalie! What are you doing? Come back!" Tori whisper-yelled from their staging area at the other end of the runway.

Finally, Natalie snapped to. She turned around,

plastered the smile back on her face, and walked back over to her friends. She was not going to let Lainie and Christopher mess this up, too. She owed it to Tori to get it right.

Back at the oak tree, Natalie squeezed Tori's hand and Tori walked out for the big finale. She was dressed up as Dr. Steve. Natalie and her friends had spent most of the morning cutting up Natalie's red T-shirt and Alex's blue one, then sewing the halves together to make Dr. Steve's Color War wardrobe. They had done the same with Grace's red New Jersey Devils shorts (which she swore her mother was going to kill her for) and Natalie's blue Ralph Lauren sport shorts, and then colored in Tori's white sneakers with paint and markers to make them blue and red. Tori had shoved her hair up under a Camp Lakeview cap to complete the look. As she walked down the runway now, she completely looked the part, and the camp erupted with laughter. Tori blew her whistle and lifted her clipboard, both of which she'd stolen from Belle's room.

"Color War is a grand tradition, people!" she shouted, lowering her voice an octave. "A grand tradition! And I expect you to take it seriously!"

She walked the rest of the runway to wild applause, then came back and pulled all her friends out from behind their tree to take a bow. As Natalie clasped Tori's hand and took in all the laughing, cheering faces, she completely forgot about Lainie and Christopher and the sixth-division girls. All that mattered was Tori's grin and the squeeze of her hand. Everything was back to the way it should be.

"Can I have your attention, please?" Tori called out, her heart pounding a mile a minute. She was so nervous and excited at the same time, she didn't know which way was up. The crowd noise died down, and she stepped into the middle of the runway, facing the judges, all of whom were front and center.

"We know this was not a traditional arts and crafts presentation, but it was a little like theater, which falls into the arts. Plus we used all the skills we learned helping put together costumes for the camp productions over the years, so that falls into crafts. We hope you agree, because this was all we ever really wanted to do. When we thought about Camp Lakeview and how to best represent it, we realized that it wasn't about the lake or the cabins or any of that stuff. While we love all of it, we know that what really makes Camp Lakeview the special place it is are the people."

At this, the entire camp roared their approval. Tori was so taken by surprise, she almost tripped backward at the noise, but instead, she laughed.

"Well, hopefully you'll take *that* into consideration when you're deciding our scores," Tori said to Dr. Steve and the other judges, earning a laugh from the crowd. "Thank you."

As she ventured back to her friends, she got another round of applause and was so giddy she couldn't keep herself from jumping up and down as she hugged them.

"You did an incredible job, Tori," Alex said.

"They all loved it."

"*We* did an incredible job," Tori corrected.

"Looks like we're about to find out if the powers that be think so, too," Natalie said, nodding past Tori.

Heart in her throat, Tori turned around to face the judges. Dr. Steve, Helene, and Jeremy paused in front of Tori, with Belle hovering just behind, clearly anxious to hear what the judges thought. Dr. Steve looked Tori up and down, one eyebrow raised.

"Interesting ensemble you have there, Tori," he commented.

Tori swallowed hard. "Well, you *are* a fashion icon, Dr. Steve," she said with a straight face.

He smirked. "I just wanted to tell you your scores personally," he told her. "We've consulted on it and we've all decided to give you full marks."

Tori felt all the breath go right out of her. "What?"

"That's right. Ten points for execution, ten for creativity, and certainly ten for representation of Camp Lakeview," Helene said with a grin.

"Oh my gosh!" Tori cried as all her friends squealed and hugged. "Thank you *so* much!"

"No, thank you," Dr. Steve said. "That was the most I've been entertained around here in years."

Dr. Steve winked at the girls, then walked away with the other judges trailing behind him. Tori turned around and fell right into the group hug that awaited her.

"See? I told you you could do it," Belle said, joining them. Her black hair was back in a red headband and she wore her red T-shirt, as she had all week, but she had yet to betray any allegiance to one side or the other. "You played to your strengths—creativity, showmanship, and fashion—and you totally knocked them dead."

"Thanks, Belle," Tori said, beaming. "Your advice really helped."

"Well, good," Belle said. And then her face completely fell and she thrust her hand out. "Now give me back my clipboard and whistle."

Tori gulped and handed Belle's things back to her. Uh-oh. Was she about to get in trouble for stealing? That would definitely put a damper on an otherwise perfect day. But Belle merely shook her head at them, then turned around and walked away, her prized clipboard tucked firmly under her arm.

"Phew. That was close. I thought her head was going to explode," Grace said.

"I gotta change out of these jeans before they fall off," Gaby said.

"Maybe we should go back to the bunk and celebrate," Alex suggested.

"Yeah! Let's celebrate!" Candace agreed.

"I'm down with that," Tori agreed, turning for the pathway to the bunks.

"Nice work, Captain Tori," Natalie said, slinging her arm over Tori's shoulders as they walked.

Tori grinned at her friend, totally happy and relaxed for the first time in days. "Couldn't have done it without you."

chapter

# THIRTEEN

"I can't believe they caught up to us in points," Jenna grumbled to Priya as they moved toward the end of the ice cream sundae buffet. "How could they have caught up to us?"

Priya added some chocolate syrup to her bowl, which was already piled with chocolate ice cream and sprinkles. Nothing like a make-your-own-sundae buffet to help a girl forget losing an important Color War event.

"Here. Drown your sorrows in sugar," Priya told Jenna, handing her the bottle.

Jenna sighed hugely, then proceeded to dump about two cups of chocolate syrup all over her already huge sundae. Priya laughed and grabbed a spoon, then headed back to their usual table in the mess hall. Jenna, Chelsea, Alyssa, Brynn, and Valerie all trailed behind her. Tori and the rest of the Blue team were already seated at one end of the table, laughing and chowing down on their sundaes. Meanwhile, all the chairs at the other end of the table were empty.

"Hey, guys," Priya said, stopping next to

Tori and Nat, who sat across from each other at the end. "I just wanted to tell you that the fashion show was incredible. You totally deserved to win."

"Thanks," Tori said with a smile.

"Hey!" Chelsea said. "No complimenting the enemy."

"Why not? If they deserve it," Alyssa said diplomatically.

"Your diorama was beautiful, too, Alyssa," Natalie said.

"Thanks. We liked it," Jenna said with a sniff.

"So, I was thinking . . . do you guys mind if I sit down here?" Priya said, gesturing at the Blue end of the table.

For a second, no one said anything, but Chelsea scoffed. All week long, the table had been divided into a Red side and a Blue side.

"Not at all," Tori said. She looked at Alex, who was next to her. "Do you mind scooting down?"

"No problem," Alex said with a grin.

She, Grace, and Tori each slid down one chair, and Priya took the seat vacated by Tori. "I feel like I haven't talked to you guys in *ages*."

"Tell me about it," Valerie said. Candace and Gaby moved over to make room for Val as well. "What's up with you guys?"

"Well, we caught up to you in points," Gaby said, all superior.

"Yeah, we heard that already," Brynn told her, dropping down next to Grace.

"Wait, wait, wait!" Jenna announced. She placed

her sundae bowl on the table and threw up her hands. "Are we really doing this? Are we really socializing with the enemy?"

Priya looked up at her. "YES!" she said in unison with a bunch of other girls.

Jenna stared at them all for a moment, then shrugged. "Okay. Just checking." Then she pulled a chair over from another table and sat at the head of the table.

Soon everyone was mixed in together, Red-Blue-Red-Blue, laughing and chatting. Priya beamed at her friends. Maybe Color War would have to continue later at the singdown, but for now, it was nice to see everyone back together again.

▲ ▲ ▲

"You guys ready to sing?" Grace asked Tori and Natalie, throwing her arms around their necks from behind as they walked to the lake. "Maybe we should do some scales. Do . . . re . . . mi . . . fa!"

Her voice cracked and Natalie winced. "Maybe you should save it for the singdown," she said, patting her friend on the back.

Grace touched her throat and swallowed. "That kind of hurt."

Natalie laughed and glanced over her shoulder at Lainie and the other sixth-division girls, who were walking a few yards behind them. Lainie stared her down and Natalie's heart clenched, but instead of quickly glancing away, she lifted her hand in a wave. Let Lainie know she wasn't affected by her attitude.

Lainie looked surprised for a brief moment, then rolled her eyes.

"So, captain, what's our first song gonna be?" Natalie asked Tori.

Suddenly Christopher Logan fell into step with them, all smiles. Natalie's heart started pounding so hard, she was sure her friends could hear it. If Lainie was watching this, which Natalie was pretty sure she was, then Nat was dead.

"Hey, Lee," Christopher said.

Ugh! Why did his hair have to fall over his forehead so adorably?

"Lee?" Tori said, her eyebrows raised.

"Long story," Natalie mumbled.

"Can I talk to you for a second?" Christopher asked. "I'd pull you into the trees, but that didn't work out so well last time."

"*Last* time?" Grace said.

"Uh, I'll explain it all to you guys later," Natalie said, pulling Christopher off to the side before he could say anything else. Grace and Tori stopped for a second to gape at them, but finally kept walking. "What do you want?" Natalie asked Christopher flatly. Lainie and her friends stormed past, giving Natalie so many death glares she was surprised she didn't just stop breathing right then and there.

"Whoa. What's with the nasty?" Christopher asked, raising his hands in surrender. "I just wanted to see if you wanted to hang out during the singdown."

"Aren't you hanging out with Lainie?" Natalie asked.

He blinked. "No."

"That's not what she said," Natalie told him.

"Okay, I have no idea what you're talking about, but you told me you couldn't hang out with me because you and Lainie were friends, right?" Christopher said. "And from what I hear, you're not friends anymore, so . . ."

"Yeah, but you two *are*," Natalie said.

"No. We're not."

"Please! I saw you guys talking during the fashion show today!" Natalie told him. "You looked pretty cozy then."

"Oh!" Christopher said, understanding lighting his handsome face. "So you must have seen us *before* she told me off. Because afterward, nobody was cozy, believe me."

Natalie blinked. She was so surprised she actually took a sideways step to get her balance. "She . . . she told you off?"

Christopher nodded. "Yeah. Right about the time I told her I liked you."

There went Natalie's breath again. "Really?"

"Lee, you're funny, you're confident, you're kind. You blow every other girl at this camp out of the water," Christopher said, reaching for her hand. "Even when you're drowning under a kayak."

Natalie laughed and her heart felt light as the breeze in the trees above them.

"So, what do you say?" he asked, lacing his fingers through hers. "Wanna be my girlfriend?"

The grin on Natalie's face was so wide it hurt.

"Sure. Under one condition."

"What's that?" Christopher asked.

"Can I please call you Logan? 'Cause in my head, Christopher is just the guy Lainie likes, and there is *way* too much negativity there."

Christopher grinned. "You can call me whatever you want. Except Tomatohead, because that's what my brother calls me and I really hate it."

"Tomatohead?" Natalie asked with a laugh.

"Yeah. I'll tell you all about it sometime," Logan told her. "How about right now, we go sing the pants off some Red teamers?"

"Sounds like a plan," Natalie said.

Logan squeezed her hand and held it all the way to the campfire. Natalie was bubbling over with happiness. She knew that once Lainie found out about this she was in for the freak-out of the century—even if Lainie *had* told Logan off—but she could deal with that later. For now, she just wanted to be happy. The moment she and Logan arrived at the clearing, Tori stepped out to meet them.

"Hey, Tori! This is Logan, my boyfriend," Natalie said giddily. Tori's eyebrows shot up at the use of the word "boyfriend," but she let it go. "Logan, this is Tori, my best friend."

"Ah, the best friend. I'm honored to meet the person Lee is going to talk about me with nonstop," Logan joked.

"And I'm honored to meet the person I'll never stop hearing about for the rest of the summer," Tori joked back.

They both smiled, and for the first time all week, Natalie felt right at home. From now on, she wasn't going to go near any sixth-division girls ever again. Well, until next summer, anyway—when she and all her friends would *be* sixth-division girls.

"All right, Camp Lakeview! Let's sing!" Dr. Steve called out.

"Woo-hoo!" Natalie cheered with the rest of the camp. She had a feeling that tonight, she was going to sing her head off.

▲ ▲ ▲

Dear Michael,

You're never going to believe it . . . THE BLUE TEAM WON! We killed at the singdown and then took the kickball tournament the following morning when Natalie—who as you know is _not_ one to sweat—actually sprinted for an outfield ball and then _dove_ to catch it for the final out! Winning that game was all we needed to put us ahead in points. We only won by five, which means that our big arts and crafts win definitely helped put us over the top! My idea contributed to the win! How cool is that?

Okay, so I lost my voice singing and I totally missed the ball every time I tried to kick it, which was totally humiliating, but it was all worth it. And you know what? I think I actually kind of like Color War.

Just don't tell anyone.

GO BLUE TEAM!


Tori

Turn the page for a sneak preview of

# camp CONFIDENTIAL

Freaky Tuesday

available soon!

# chapter ONE

**Posted by: Brynn**
**Subject: Heeelp!!!!**

My whole life has been flipped upside down. No,
make that my whole WORLD. And I'm not just being
my usual drama-girl self. Really. First, I get home
from camp and I have a whole different house. My
parents moved over the summer. Without telling
me. They said they thought it would be a—note the
quotes—"fun surprise." Hello. Surprises are excellent
for birthdays, not major life changes.

Actually, after I got over the shock—Hey, that's what
my parents should have called it. A "fun shock."
Anyway, after I adjusted, I decided the new place
is pretty cool. It's not that far away from where we
used to live. And my new room—it has shutters on the
inside. Cute white shutters. I LOOOOVE them. They are
so much more original than curtains or blinds. And
my parents are letting me redecorate. I'm getting
one of those beds that has curtains draped all around
it. Not a canopy. But like a gauzy tent. And, yes, I

know I just basically said curtains are uncool. But that's just on windows. Around a bed—they're fabulous!

Anyway, the new house with the new room and the new furniture is only part of the life flipping. I'm also going to a new school. A private one, with uniforms and everything. Confession—I'm scared!!!

I've never been the new girl before. I know I'm not exactly shy or anything, but I have a little case of the wiggins thinking about walking into my first class not knowing anybody. As in ANYbody. Have any of you ever been the new girl? If you have, heeelp! I need survival tips. Who do I sit with at lunch on the all-important Day One? Am I supposed to start up conversations with people before classes start? Or do I wait and let them talk to me first, since I'm the newb? What if I get lost and have to walk into class late? What do I say? Please advise.

And that advising, I need it fast, fast, fast. 'Cause I have to start at my new school the Tuesday after Labor Day. I always thought private schools started later. So please, please, please answer before then.

Brynn stared at her computer screen, willing one of her Camp Lakeview buddies to post an answer on their blog. Maybe Grace. She was always so calm and rational. Or Natalie. She'd walked down the red carpet on her way to the Oscars with her dad. She'd definitely know how to handle a minor social situation like how to deal with a new school.

*You were popular at your old school. You'll be popular at your new school,* Brynn told herself. But she still wanted the assist from her friends. Just to be on the safe side.

She checked her computer to see if any answers had come in during the fourteen seconds since she posted her message. Nope. But there were a few messages she hadn't read yet. She clicked on the most recent one from Gaby Parsons. Gaby wasn't her favorite Camp Lakeview girl, but she did have a snarky sense of humor. She'd probably have something entertaining to say. Brynn started to read.

**Posted by: Gaby**
**Subject: Sainthood**

This goes out to everyone who lives around Philadelphia. I'm going to be volunteering at the Home Away From Home center near the Children's Hospital and I wanted to know if any of you would like to volunteer with me. Home Away From Home is a place where the families of sick kids can stay while the kids are in the hospital.

I decided that this year I want to spend more time thinking about other people. That whole situation at camp where I sort of fibbed to all of you? Okay, I mean I told you big fat lies. That time? The way you were all so nice to me afterward made me think that maybe I should try and be a little nicer. So what do you say? I'll be in charge and get things organized. Come on, don't you want to be good like me? From now on, I expect you all to call me Saint Gabrielle.

*Huh*, Brynn thought. *Good for Gaby*. Brynn's world had gotten shaken up by her parents moving and deciding Brynn should go to private school. But Gaby was shaking up her own life because she wanted to be a better person. That was pretty cool.

Brynn did a check for new messages again, because now it had been more than a minute since she'd posted her plea for heeelp. And this time there were two—one from Valerie and one from Alex. Brynn read Valerie's first.

**Posted by: Valerie**
**Subject: Chill**

Brynn, don't be stressing. You HAVE been the new girl once already, and it went great! Think about it—you were the new girl your first year at camp. We were all newbs. We didn't even know why you shouldn't eat the meat loaf. And we came away from our first summer with tons of BFFs. Look at us. We're all hanging out on the board, keeping in touch. So I repeat, there's no need for stress!

P.S. Wilmer Valderrama rocks my socks!

*Good point*, Brynn thought. *We were all camp new girls. And camp turned out so fun!* Already feeling better about her first day as the new girl, Brynn moved on to Alex's post.

**Posted by: Alex**
**Subject: Brynn Friends**

I have advice, Brynn. I have the perfect advice. All you have to do is join the drama club. You're so talented. They're going to be so happy to have you as soon as they see you do your stuff. I bet after one meeting you'll have more friends at your new school than you can handle. That's how it was for me once I started joining different sports.

Good luck! And you better not forget about me when all those new friends of yours are always calling you!

By the time Brynn finished reading Alex's message, a post from Grace had popped up on the board. Her camp friends were *so* coming through for her! She clicked on Grace's post and started to read.

**Posted by: Grace**
**Subject: Drama Queens Rule (tee-hee)**

Of course drama club is the answer! We both know how tight drama people are. You'll have oodles of friends in days.

I gotta go. It's garbage night and my mom is yelling for me to take out the trash. If you are still feeling stressed, do what I do—eat twelve purple gummy bears. Yes, they have to be purple or it won't work.

Brynn smacked herself on the forehead. Alex and Grace were so right! Brynn already had friends at her new school. Drama friends. They just hadn't met her yet. And she hadn't met them. But they were still her friends. Once she met them, they'd introduce her to their non-drama friends, and Wilton Academy popularity, here Brynn came.

▲ ▲ ▲

*This is SO nothing like the first day of camp,* Brynn thought as she stepped through the heavy oak doors that led into the Wilton Academy. At camp, the counselors had getting-to-know you games planned. They made sure all the kids got introduced to one another, and that nobody was left out.

There were no camp-counselor types here. She was on her own. *Just remember what Alex and Grace said about drama club,* Brynn reminded herself. *That will change things.*

She checked her watch. Fifteen minutes before her first class. She couldn't just stand at her locker looking like the loneliest girl on the planet. The bathroom, she decided. She could brush her hair, do a lip gloss check, and make sure the tie on her blue plaid uniform wasn't askew. That would keep her busy.

But first she had to find the bathroom. One of the other new-girl things. She didn't know where anything was. She could ask someone, but everyone seemed to be talking to somebody already, doing the catching-up-after-summer-vacay thing.

Brynn decided to just head down the hall and

keep her eyes open. And before she'd reached the corner, there it was—the ladies' room. She stepped inside and headed over to the sinks. Three girls were already clustered in front of the mirrors, gabbing away.

She thought about the message Natalie had posted on the blog that morning. She'd said not to worry about who talked first. She'd told Brynn that if she felt like talking, she should just talk. *Curtain up! Showtime!* she told herself. "Hi," she said brightly as she searched her purse for her favorite peach lip gloss. "I'm new here. Just moved into the area, even though I've always lived around Boston. So, what's the club situation at this school? When do they start up?"

The tallest girl gave Brynn a friendly smile. "There'll be sign-up tables in the caf starting tomorrow at lunch," she answered. "What club are you thinking of?"

"Drama," Brynn answered. "I live for the stage!" she exclaimed, vamping it up for added effect. The tall girl wrinkled her nose a little. Like Brynn had let out a big smelly burp in her face.

"Do we even have a drama club here?" one of the other girls asked doubtfully, trying to straighten the knot in her tie.

*How could there not be? What kind of school wouldn't have a drama club?* Brynn thought. She ran her fingers through her dark red hair, fluffing it up.

"There is one. That girl Iris was in it last year," the first girl said.

"Oh, right. Icky Iris." The third girl smoothed down her bangs and stepped away from the mirrors.

"She was upgraded," the girl who'd been fiddling with her tie jumped in. "She became Irritating Iris, remember?"

All three girls laughed. The tall girl turned to Brynn. "There's definitely a drama club."

Brynn nodded. "Thanks."

The tall girl turned back to her friends. "How many of the books on the summer reading list did you get through?"

"All of them, of course," the girl with the now perfect tie answered.

Brynn's throat went a little dry. "Um, what class had assigned summer reading?"

"It's not for a particular class," the tall girl explained. "Each grade has a reading list. We're all supposed to read five books from it. Samantha just likes to be better than everybody else." She gave perfect-tie girl a playful slap on the shoulder.

"Like you didn't read them all," the girl, Samantha, teased her back. "You're way too competitive not to have. You might end up with an A-minus or something." She glanced at Brynn. "Didn't your old school have summer reading?"

Brynn shook her head.

"I'm sure you'll be able to catch up," the tall girl told her as she and her friends headed out of the bathroom.

*Catch up? It's only day one,* Brynn thought.

The first bell rang, and she hurried out of the bathroom. After Grace had taken out the trash, she'd posted another message on the blog advising Brynn how to deal if she got lost and ended up being late to class. It was advice Brynn didn't want to have to use.

She found her history classroom with a full three minutes to spare. Three minutes to start making some BFFs. Or at least Fs.

The problem was, everyone in the room was already talking to somebody else. Except one girl who was reading a massive book. Was the book something that had been on that reading list? The one Brynn knew nothing about?

Slowly, Brynn unloaded her history book, her binder, a pen, and a pencil from her backpack. Carefully, she arranged them on her desk. That had taken . . . not even an entire minute.

Now what? Everyone was still talking—or reading. Brynn's face started to feel like a mask.

She forced a smile. Then she immediately turned the corners of her lips down. What kind of loser sat around smiling into space? Except frowning into space wasn't any better. That definitely wouldn't make her look like somebody it would be fun to be Fs with.

Brynn pressed her lips together, then tried to hold them in a nice, even line. For some reason the effort made her jaw ache. She wanted to waggle it back and forth, but that would look weird. Looking weird was worse than looking like somebody who wasn't any fun.

Finally, the teacher walked in and about fifteen seconds later, the second bell rang. Brynn didn't think she'd ever been so happy for class to start.

"Hello, everyone. For those of you who don't

know me, I'm Ms. Owen. I know you probably all have a little case of whiplash. Yesterday was vacation. Today school. So I thought we'd kick things off with something fun. A few rounds of History Bowl." She clapped her hands. "Volunteers for team captain."

Every single hand in the room—except Brynn's—went up.

"Okay, let's go with Eve and Peter," Ms. Owen said.

"I get Colin," a boy Brynn assumed was Peter called out.

"No fair!" the other captain, Eve, shot back. "Colin even sleeps with the History Channel on."

"You get the next pick, Eve," Ms. Owen told her.

Eve scanned the room quickly. "Maddy."

"Good choice," the guy behind Brynn muttered. "I live next door to Maddy, and she spent all summer making flash cards."

*You're kidding me*, Brynn thought. *All summer? Who does that?*

"I made flashcards, too," the girl who'd been reading commented.

*I guess that answers my question*, Brynn thought.

Peter and Eve kept calling out names. And it suddenly hit Brynn that she was going to be the last kid picked.

*It doesn't mean anything*, she told herself. *How could either of them pick you? They don't even know your name.*

Suddenly, Eve pointed to Brynn.

"What's your GPA?" Eve asked.

"Umm . . ." Brynn stuttered. She wasn't exactly sure. She'd never bothered to figure it out.

"Eve, that question was not appropriate," Ms. Owen said firmly.

"I'll take Rick," Eve decided.

Peter looked around the room. Brynn knew she was the only one who hadn't been chosen. It took him a second longer. "I'll take—"

"Brynn," she supplied.

"Great," the boy behind her muttered. "Couldn't have been anything decent or she would have said."

*At least there's one place where GPAs and what books you've read—or haven't—don't matter,* Brynn thought as she stepped into the cafeteria.

As she moved through the food line, grabbing a taco and fruit salad, she promised herself she was going to talk to at least one person before lunch was over. But which person? She scoped out the tables, deciding against the ones that were already almost full. The ones that were basically empty didn't seem right, either. There had to be a reason they were avoided, right?

She picked one that was about half full and had a couple of kids she recognized from her morning classes sitting at it, including the girl who'd been reading the massive book before history. "Hi," she said as she took one of the empty seats. She got hi's from pretty much everyone except one boy, who just grunted. He was already working on his homework as he shoveled food into his mouth.

"I'm Brynn. I just started here," she offered.

"Cool," the book girl said. Then she pulled out her ginormous book and started to read.

"How's everybody's first day back starting out?" Brynn asked no one in particular.

This time she got grunts from everyone. They were all either reading or scribbling away on homework as they ate. This was craziness.

*There has to be a table that's more fun,* Brynn thought. She looked around the room.

Her jaw dropped open. She didn't believe what she was seeing. It couldn't be possible.

She leaned forward and squinted. "This is just too bizarre," she whispered. No one at her table bothered to ask her what she was talking about.

Brynn grabbed her backpack and her lunch tray and stood up. She needed a much closer look. "Bye, you guys," she said, and got some grunts back.

Her day seemed like it was going to turn around. There was actually somebody she knew at this school! Somebody who was already a friend! Maybe not a BFF, but definitely an F.

Of all the people in the entire world, Candace—repeats-every-phrase-ever-uttered-to-her Candace—was sitting at a table about twenty feet away from her. Never mind that she and Brynn had never actually passed the acquaintance stage—Brynn raced over to her as if they'd been long lost friends, and then waited for a pause in the group conversation.

"You run for president, and I'll run for vice

president," Samantha, the girl who had been fiddling with her tie in the bathroom, told Candace. "We'll be unstoppable. And if you hold a class office in middle school, it's easier to do it in high school. People just see you as a leader. And being a class officer in high school is great college-application material."

"I'd vote for the two of you," a cute blond boy said.

Suddenly, Brynn got it. Candace was one of the popular kids. Capital P popular. Class president popular.

Talk about bizarre. Not only was Candace a student at Brynn's new school, she was popular there. Shy, awkward, Candace.

"I'd vote for you, too, Candace," Brynn volunteered, jumping into the conversation.

Candace looked over her shoulder and her eyes widened. "Brynn!"

Samantha raised her eyebrows. "Do you two know each other?"

"We go to the same camp," Brynn explained. "And now we go to the same school, too!"

"You're going to school with me?" Candace said, doing a little of her echo thing.

"Yep," Brynn answered. She waited for Candace to ask her to sit down. There was one empty seat.

But Candace just kept looking at her.

"Anyway, I just wanted to say hi," Brynn finally said lamely. "I'll see you around." She gave a little wave to the group. Then she walked away, trying to decide if she should go back to the table of grunters or find a new place to sit.

*Is there anyplace I'm going to fit in here?* she asked herself.

She wasn't sure about the answer. How could she be sure of anything when Candace was one of the popular kids? The Wilton Academy was turning out to be some bizarre backward school.

How was she going to survive?